PUFF

A Grue

Barbara Griffiths studied at the Slade in London and on her graduation had an acclaimed exhibition at a London art gallery. *A Gruesome Body* is the first book she has written and illustrated in her exquisite, surreal style.

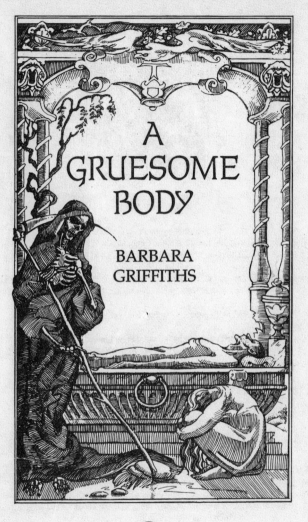

A
GRUESOME
BODY

BARBARA
GRIFFITHS

PUFFIN BOOKS

For Jeremy

PUFFIN BOOKS

Published by the Penguin Group
Penguin Books Ltd, 27 Wrights Lane, London W8 5TZ, England
Penguin Books USA Inc., 375 Hudson Street, New York, New York 10014, USA
Penguin Books Australia Ltd, Ringwood, Victoria, Australia
Penguin Books Canada Ltd, 10 Alcorn Avenue, Toronto, Ontario, Canada M4V 3B2
Penguin Books (NZ) Ltd, 182–190 Wairau Road, Auckland 10, New Zealand

Penguin Books Ltd, Registered Offices: 'Harmondsworth, Middlesex, England

First published by Andersen Press Limited 1994
Published in Puffin Books 1996
1 3 5 7 9 10 8 6 4 2

Contents

CYBERSLAYER III

The first thing you need when planning a trip to the cinema is a one-day travel card. That, and a *Time Out*. Me and Chris had decided to see the new Schwarzenegger 'At a Cinema near you NOW! (Cert. 15)'; but as we all know, your nearest cinema may not be your dearest.

'Fifteen? You two? Don't make me laugh, boys. Come back when you're out of nappies.'

So we cut the locals and took the bus to the multiplex at Staples Corner. There was a queue right round the car park, so we took another two buses to the Holloway Odeon. Chris said, 'Perhaps we should try again next week. I mean, everyone goes to see it on the first day. We haven't got a chance.'

'There's no point at all if we don't see it this weekend. I can just hear Rex and his mates on Monday: "Seen *Cyberslayer III* yet? No? Well, I don't suppose they'd let you in, would they? You don't know what you're missing. It's the *best* film *ever*." '

Chris groaned. 'Yeah. And then they'll tell us the plot.'

'In cyberslaying detail,' I said.

We'd struck lucky at Holloway before, but today there was a new girl on the till.

'We *are* fifteen,' we grovelled. 'Honest. Oh, go on. Please.'

'Well . . .' She considered. 'I'll see what the manager says. Just wait there.'

So we stood by the poster, admiring the way the flesh of the Cyberslayer's cheekbones melts into that lethal metal jawbone, with the blades for teeth.

'How much hardware can a human add without becoming a cybernaut?' I asked. 'I mean, how do you differentiate?'

'Oh, that's easy,' Chris said. 'Cybernauts don't have empathy.'

I thought about this. 'In that case, how do you tell Rex and his gang from cybernauts? Or anyone in our form?'

I had him there.

'If we don't get in,' I said, 'it'll be your fault. That's a really lame haircut. Makes you look about ten.'

'At least I've had my thirteenth birthday,' Chris said. 'That's more than you can – '

I felt a fist grab my collar, and we were hurled through the doors. From the steps we watched the manager's back as he strode away, rubbing his hands together.

'That's not very sporting,' I grumbled. 'Hanging about eavesdropping. How were we supposed to know he was the manager?'

'On with the quest,' said Chris, flicking through the *Time Out*. 'Crouch End Palace is our best bet.'

'Too sleazy,' I said.

'They'll be glad of our money, then, won't they?'

I'll bet there's one cinema somewhere in the suburbs, if only we could find it, full of blissful infants sucking away at their dummies in front of an (18) movie. Trouble is, word of mouth is the only way to find out about these places, and with so many boastful liars around, that's very unreliable.

We set off towards the tube station. The sun was battering down on us, and I was getting bad-tempered. I can't think why parents are always on at you to get out in the fresh air, when all any self-respecting child wants to do in the summer is to avoid daylight; D and D caves, bowling alleys, arcades and lazerdromes are a child's natural habitat.

'Don't look back,' Chris whispered, 'but I think we're being followed. I said *don't* look!'

A man in black hat and raincoat was gazing in a shop window.

'What makes you think he's following us?' I asked.

'He was at Staples Corner.'

'Crap. It was probably someone else. Looks a pretty average guy to me.'

'Average! When did you last see someone in a hat and coat in August? With an umbrella, too!'

I admit I hadn't noticed the umbrella.

'A foreign tourist, no doubt,' I said, 'playing safe.'

We ran down the steps into the tube station and fed our tickets through the automatic barrier. Overtaking the travellers on the escalator, we clattered to the bottom. I glanced up and saw a solitary hat among the bare heads. We ran along the tunnel, trailing up the sides and down again, onto the platform.

'Totteridge,' read the electronic sign, 'one minute.' I stuck my head back round the corner, and through the bobbing mass again saw the man in the hat. His umbrella was furled, its curved handle swinging on his wrist as he bent to drop a coin into the busker's guitar case. He did a little dance.

'Seems like a nice guy,' I said, then shouted, 'Anyway, he'll never make the train.' With a gush of wind, the train thrust from the tunnel. We got in and scrambled for a seat.

'Wanna bet?' said Chris, peering through the swaying slabs of glass between carriages.

'Stop fussing like an old gran,' I said. 'What you should be bothered about is whether we make the 5.05 showing.'

We sprinted through the streets like the undead caught short at dawn. At the top of a hill, rearing up between a kebab house and a laundrette, we came upon THE PA ACE. The regal name fluttered in pink neon up its crumbling Art Deco cliff-face. A sign by the door read, 'Acquired by Officepride Developments'. There was no queue.

'It's closed down,' said Chris. He looked ready to cry.

'Can't be. They've got the poster.' I pushed the heavy door, and it creaked open. The foyer seemed empty. Then we heard 'click click, click click' from the cash desk. Leaning over it, I found an old woman knitting.

'Please could we have two tickets for *Cyberslayer III*, please,' I said.

'How old are you, dear?'

'I'm . . . well, I'm fourteen.'

She shook her head reproachfully. Give her a

shawl, I thought, and she'd be that peasant in Dracula films who always says, 'Nay, young master, tha dursn't stray in these parts after dark.'

'Nasty,' she told us. 'Real gory, it is. We've got *Cock-a-Doodle-Dandy* next week. Disney. You'll like that.'

'Give us a break. We've come all the way from Bushey!'

'Well, I don't know . . . You go in quick, then. But no screaming, mind, or the manager'll have me bones for breakfast.'

We seized the tickets and made for the front row. The commercials were already rolling. I put my hands on my lap so as not to touch the armrests – I suspect that they never put the lights on in pits like the Palace to save on cleaning, and there's always a smell of sick and cigarettes. I'd already trodden on something sticky. I could hear sweet papers rustling under my seat, and told myself it wasn't rats – just the draught from the door. I swivelled and saw a shape in its bright oblong.

'He's here,' I whispered to Chris.

The light narrowed, and black slipped into black in a seat at the far corner of the cinema.

'See, I told you,' Chris muttered. 'He's after us.'

'We're big boys now. We can look after ourselves. Shh, it's starting.'

The titles swooped over skyscrapers, and then the camera closed in at street level. I leaned forwards, chewing my nails; I was feeling the way you do when the TV announcer says, 'Some viewers may find these scenes distressing', or, better still, 'We are leaving for a newsflash.' Two characters were sauntering down the sidewalk. Unfamous faces, I thought gleefully, and acting happy; they

11

won't last long. A shadow slid across the road and zigzagged up the kerb. My heart was going like a drum solo. Why didn't they look behind them?

Chris nudged me. 'What's that?'

'Sound effects,' I said.

'It's not the film,' said Chris, and we looked back into the cinema. Now our eyes were used to the dark, we could see the graveyard outline of empty seats.

The man had moved diagonally nearer and was sitting about ten rows back. He was gobbling popcorn from a large carton, stuffing it into the shade under the hat brim; fragments shattered, exploding sideways. His head was sunk into his shoulders till the hat rested on them, and the white-gloved hand moved steadily from box to shadow, box to shadow. He must have seen us watching him, for the hand hovered, then shot upwards and waved.

I made a disgusted grimace at Chris, and turned back to the screen. The Cyberslayer was catching up with the couple; his bladed claw flexed in readiness.

Chris nudged me again.

'Look, will you shut up? We're getting to the good bit!' I hissed.

'He's closing in on us.'

I glanced over my shoulder again; the creep was five rows away. He took his hand from the carton and rippled the fingers at me in a small salute.

'Just ignore him,' I said.

'I think we should tell the manager.'

'Tell him what? We haven't even been offered a sweetie yet.'

'I don't care. I'm scared.' He started to stand up, but I pushed him down again.

'Don't be such a dweeb. All the manager'll do is chuck us out for being under age. If he doesn't phone our parents. Or the police! Now *shush*.'

I'd missed the g.b., and you always have to wait twenty minutes for another – it was all over bar the red puddle on the tarmac.

The scene shifted to a suburban home, where a baby plays in the back-yard sandpit. The doorbell rings and the mother runs to answer it.

'Sorry to trouble you, ma'am,' drawls the cop, 'but we've reason to believe the Cyberslayer is operatin' in this neighbourhood . . .' The camera tracks to the back yard, where the baby, naturally, is crawling out of the gate . . .

I felt a touch on my shoulder and, looking down, saw, like a row of slugs, four white fingers.

'Get *off*!' I said.

The white-gloved hand fluttered away, and there was a moist sigh from under the hat. 'I merely wished to offer you some popcorn.'

I jumped out of my seat, which sprang up loudly, and moved to the end of the row. Chris followed me.

'Let's leave,' he begged, 'it's not such a brilliant film, anyway.'

'Oh yes, it is. I admit the creep does a good imitation of a serial killer, but I'm not impressed. I'll tell you what he is. He's an inadequate person who makes himself feel big by scaring little kids.'

'Do you believe in ghosts?' The voice slithered between our shoulders.

'No!' I said. 'Shut up.'

'Are you a ghost?' Chris asked, without turning his head. I could see sweat glistening on his nose. Violent images writhed in red reflection on his

14

fixed, shiny eyes.

'Not I. But I'd really like to tell you about them.'

'Shh,' I said, and whispered to Chris, 'He's the worst sort of cinema pest – someone who talks, eats popcorn and wears a hat.' I felt a waft of breath lap my ear.

'Ghosts, my dears, as I was just explaining, are the bloody fingerprints of tragedy upon the scene of its enactment . . .'

I moved five seats to the right, and Chris followed. So did the voice.

'. . . whereas I,' it went on, 'you might say, am more of an emanation. When these gold rays dance, you see, on dark, the stink of fear rises, fair steams off the watchers . . . swirls syrupy in the shifting light shaft, so thick that spirits solidify, swim to haunt these halls of myth. And we spirits feed on the fear that makes us. We seek out, suck the sweet terror of the watchers – and the younger the watcher, the *eeeEEA*sier he scares!'

I heard Chris's seat bang, and saw him scrambling along the row, running for the exit.

'Wait!' I cried, and tumbled after him, catching the door as it swung in my face. The cashier nodded in satisfaction as we crashed through the foyer. 'Told you it were nasty!'

'Calm down,' I said, catching Chris's sleeve as we ran down the steps. 'The guy's just a weirdo.'

His eyes were bright, the skin scraped dark around them. There was a curve of red dashes on his lower lip where he'd bitten it.

'Don't worry. It was a lame film, anyway,' I comforted him. 'Come on. Let's get you home.'

We started to walk down the hill. I looked back. It was sundown, and a triangle of shadow bisected the cinema, obscuring the doors; all I could make out were the pink letters.

'I can't see him,' I said and, despite myself, shuddered. 'Let's run.'

It's strange how every suburb is a foreign country, the houses on a different scale, the colour of the bricks, of the people, unfamiliar. Here on the hill the sun pressed close, squeezing our shadows to jigsaw shapes. Hardware, video, optician were behind us; grocer's, newsagent, minicab lay ahead, and then the tube. There was a sour taste in my mouth; the traffic din throbbed in my ears to the rhythm of my panting. I coughed and bent over, holding my knees. My entire body shook to the pounding of my heart.

'You can't stop now!' Chris shouted. Floating down the hill behind us came the humped bat-shape of the umbrella.

I spat and straightened, trying to find my cool. 'Don't be such a worrywart,' I said.

Chris took my wrist and tugged me into the tiled entrance of the tube station. I shook his hand off and started going through my pockets for our travel cards – I've got so much stuff, like video cards, special-offer pizza coupons – but I found them, and started prising off the chewing gum so they'd go in the barrier machine. I never saw someone literally wring their hands before.

'For Gawd's sake, Chris,' I said, 'I'm being as fast as I can.' His hands clenched.

'How can I keep pace,' a voice dripped, 'with boys so fleet of foot? Why, I might have lost you!'

'Get lost yourself!' I said, not looking up, getting my thumbnail under the gum. 'Or I'll report you.'

'You may, if you so wish; though I am invisible

to others less vulnerable, less sensitive than your-selves. They may well mock. Far better to take me home. Regard me, perhaps, as the stray cat who moves in; or, closer still, the ivy on the church tower – a slight infection of the blood, even.'

'I'm not scared of you,' I said, giving Chris his ticket. 'Why don't you show your face?'

'No,' said Chris, 'please, no.'

The thing shrank back slightly. 'I cannot face the light, for I come from light, and would dissolve in that element. My face, besides, is the distillation of every horror ever screened; you would not wish to see it.'

I've always believed that no horrors are as bad as those we imagine.

'Ah, yes,' murmured the creature, imbibing my thoughts. 'But I am in your imagination, and made by it.'

I put my hand out, and faltered. Then I took a breath and reached again, clawing at the hat, the scarf, the dark glasses. My hand plunged, unre-sisted, through the apparition.

'You see?' it crowed. 'I am the projection of your fear.'

'If I see you unmasked,' I challenged, 'and if I'm not scared, you will vanish.'

'A fair bargain,' it tittered, 'but you will die of terror, little boy, let me tell you that. I am beyond nightmare.'

'Don't be an idiot,' Chris whimpered.

'There's no choice,' I said. 'And if you are a film creature, as you say, a sort of phantom of the cinema, this is how we'll do it.'

I walked over to the booth for passport photo-graphs and wound up the stool. 'We'll have a photo of you,' I said. 'Do you know what that is? Like films, but still.'

He peered in. 'This is a pleasantly dark closet,' he remarked, 'quite similar to the tomb in *Devil's Daughter.*'

He sat down.

'That's right,' I said, pulling the little orange curtain across. 'You can show your face now.'

Below the curtain, we could see the trousers crease at the knees, shifting in and out of focus, the raincoat coiling behind. We saw the white gloves, deft as a mime artist's, fold the scarf upon the knees, place the hat upon the scarf, prop the sunglasses around the hat brim.

'Now!' Chris whispered. 'Let's run.'

'Not yet,' I said, and put two pounds into the slot; I pressed the button.

Whatever's behind the curtain falls still.

Flash: light flares to bleach its image. Hands fly off the knees, fingers writhe.

Flash: the hat tilts, sunglasses rattle to the floor. The knees jerk; there are several high moans. The scarf wriggles down the trouserlegs to crawl about the shoes. A foul smell reaches us.

'What's happening?' Chris cries.

'Death from exposure,' I say. 'In fact, several exposures.'

Flash: one by one the gloved fingers flop off. The coat and shoes fuse stickily, crinkling into the shoes; there they bubble, sluggishly overflowing onto the forecourt.

Flash: shoes, hat, umbrella, glasses crumble into the puddle, where maggot fingers squirm. It seethes, separates; a shimmer, a swirl, and there's just

18

a patch of dust.

Far below us a train passes, and wind rakes the floor, dragging the dust to streaks. We watch, mesmerised, as a man in overalls shuffles by, his broom sweeping crisp packets and newspapers and cigarette butts, scraping them along, mixing into the recipe about a tablespoon of granulated instant horror.

'All right for some,' he says, 'havin' a nice day off.'

We push our travel cards into the barrier, then stand on the escalator. Soberly we walk onto the platform to wait for the train.

As it draws in, a shriek echoes through the tunnel.

'Someone's had a fright,' I say, swinging on board. I smile to myself. 'I know passport photos are generally dire,' I add, 'but I'll bet those are something else!'

THE WARLORDS OF PENGE

I was keen on fantasy from an early age. It started with fairy stories, even the ones that begin, 'A certain king had seven sons, and set each seven tasks...' I moved on to the sort of stories that start, 'Only the foolhardy or the very brave would willingly risk a journey into Darkwood Forest; who knows what deadly adventures await the unwary traveller in the eerie depths and threatening shadows? Do *you* dare to enter?'

I got my big brother interested too, though he suspects it's uncool. We soon discovered adventure gaming, but I couldn't get the kids in my class to take it seriously, and Darren wouldn't even ask, in case the girls found out; so we decided to advertise for players on the Games Workshop noticeboard.

One Saturday morning we got the train to London and took a bus to the department store where the Workshop is to be found.

THE ADVENTURE STARTS HERE:

Should we: (a) go down the escalator and have a Coke?

20

(b) enter the Reject Shop, and have a look at the
   rude adult toys?

(c) go straight up to the Games Workshop?

I'm afraid this is my story, not yours, so you can't
choose. Besides, in my experience, things generally
just happen, and you don't have any choice in the
matter. As you already know, we're going to the
Workshop, so let's get on with it. The window is
always a great sight, all those dragons and warriors,
a window to gladden your heart in that dread land
of sock and sofa shops. A bit like the end of a quest,
when you've come all the way from Penge. Come
to think of it, Oxford Street already has its cast of
role-players.

Monks: equipment, robes and cymbals; chant,
'Krishna krishna, hare krishna.'

Ancient Hermit: equipment, sandwich board;
chant, 'Scourge thy flesh, eat only lentils.'

Thief: equipment, milk crate; chant, 'Stolen
goods, ladies, all stolen jewellery, yours for £10 in
a Gucci bag.'

Plus the countless hordes of beggars.

In the Workshop, by the door, there's a glass case
for painted models. I always have a look to see how
mine compare. Past the games, past the books and
before the T-shirts is the noticeboard.

There were quite a few good ones that Saturday.

We are the EMPORER'S WARRIORS. We do as he Command's to do battle against his FOE'S who will be
vanquished across the land.

'There's something threatening about them,'
Darren said.

21

I reflected. 'It's the capital letters. Makes 'em look like blackmail demands. Hey, is that one awesome, or what?'

Be it known that this fair challenge is issued to any and all Pretenders and sundry miscreants. Let the petty Tyrants and squabbling brigands come forth to meet in fair combat at a place to be appointed and may the Gods smile upon the just.
signed: His most serene Majesty,
         Defender of the just,
         Lord of the twin seas,
         Sigismundo the Nameless,
         High Duke of Phagleano.

'Nah,' said Darren. 'He's a prat. He's not nameless at all, he's Sigismundo, High Duke of Phagleano; with a Croydon phone number, so that's out.'
'Still, nice style though,' I said enviously. I pinned our ad beside it. If you include the drawing, it had taken me an hour to get right.

TO WHO THAT DARE:
We the Eliminaters send fourth a chalenge to anyone who is brave enough or belives his army to be strong enugh to combat Tuesdays, 8–10 p.m., at 65 Bexley Avenue, Penge.
Darren and Dale
THE WARLORDS OF PENGE

It looked OK. Then I bought a Blood-Axe Madboy model, and we left.
'Don't you think it's a bit risky?' Darren suggested, as we stood on the escalator.
'What?'

22

'Putting our address like that. A burglar might turn up, or a pervert, or anyone.'

'I suppose you think we should ask for references. "Excuse me, Sigismundo, your lordship, could we please see your credentials?" ' I mocked. I like to think that we fantasy role-players are a sacred brotherhood.

We'd picked Tuesday night because Mum and Dad are out; it can really cramp your style as, for instance, Wild Warrior of Chaos, if your mum comes in with a tray of cocoa. On Tuesday evening I helped Darren clear his room. There are always a week's socks on the floor, but no pants. Perhaps he never changes them. We put the table in the middle of the room and rolled out the vinyl megamap, then brought up the kitchen chairs, and crisps and fizzy drinks. By seven o'clock I was getting quite nervous in case no one turned up. By seven thirty, I was hoping they wouldn't.

I'll say one thing, though: I'm always proud of our house, when people come for the first time. Dad's got it looking lovely. It's half of a pair of semi-detached, but our half has diamond-paned triple-glazed windows (you can hardly hear the motorway at all), and the front garden is all concreted over, so we can park three cars, with chains on posts. Really smart.

I got paper and pencils, and the dice, and sat down to wait. The room looked great with just the Anglepoise shining on the table. Atmospheric's the word. I read the handbook and started getting into my character. His name is Mordred, a city rogue who lives by his wits. I've been building him up for about a year.

When the bell chimed, I ran downstairs and turned on the porch lantern. I opened the door; there were two visitors on the step.

'Greetings!' I said. 'Mordred welcomes ye, O weary strangers.' There was a podgy kid in a baseball cap and a tall guy dressed as a monk.

'Don't tell me, don't tell me,' I exclaimed, 'you must be Hemler Rottingflesh, Chaos Sorcerer of the Nurgles!' (There's a picture in the handbook.)

'No,' he replied. His voice rattled from the shady depths of his hood. 'I am the Avenger.'

He had a Kent accent you could cut with a dagger.

'And I'm Giant Lorin, Mighty Slayer of Bredith,' piped up the little kid. I think he was feeling upstaged.

'Enter,' I said, 'straight on up the stairs.' As the Avenger swept past, I admired the authentic squalor of his costume, the putrid, disintegrating robes. He wore sandals even a pottery teacher wouldn't contemplate.

'Come on the bus in that lot, did you?' I asked, as we went into Darren's room.

He didn't reply. The little kid made for the other side of the table. 'We're not together,' he said.

I introduced Darren – he plays under his own name, though you're not supposed to – and we all sat down. I explained the scenario, which was to stop the undead army engulfing Fragelhorn Valley and marching into Bretonnia. I had plotted the map myself, and the forests were wire wool sprayed green. Darren handed round the crisps, which were expensive ones, with their jackets on. The Avenger was muttering to himself, fumbling inside his robes. Suddenly he swung an arm, scraggy as a

24

vulture's wing, across the table. The dwarfholds, the Skaag hills and the Halls of Kazrad Kain, even my best war-hounds, were scattered over the carpet. He held up a large scroll.

I was quite upset, I'll admit; but when he unrolled the parchment over the table, I caught my breath. It was a map, exquisitely painted. You could see different trees in the forests, oaks and pines, and trees I don't know the names of, you could even see birds in them, and the crinkly waves on the rivers were tipped with silver. There were grasslands with sheep, and a few villages with wattle huts which were almost 3-D.

'No Cokes on the table,' said Darren, and we began to play. We decided the Avenger should be Gamesmaster, as it was his map. I felt quite ashamed of my model.

'In ancient times,' the Avenger began, 'when the world was green, the Stone Gods and their henchmen despoiled the land. A shepherd boy, high on a hill, saw them come, and set out to repel the invaders.'

He pointed at Darren, his finger jutting black against the light. 'You encounter the boy in the Valley of Larkspur. Will you fight him? Will you turn him to stone? Or will you flee to the forest?'

'Fight,' said Darren, and threw the dice. He got a 30, enough to slay the boy, and galloped off to the nearest settlement. Me and Lorin, who'd been hiding in the woods, charged along to join him, and together we burned the village to the ground. 'Razed', I think the word is. I do like being the bad guy, it's always more fun. And I make a point of always choosing the most dangerous course.

Whatever we pillaged the Avenger erased with

his sleeve, so that bright harbours and hamlets blurred to a grey smudge. Bit of a shame, really.

'This is a pushover,' said Lorin. 'I think you should make it more difficult, with dragons and things. Ogres, perhaps.'

'The Gamesmaster's always right,' Darren reminded him.

'GM, for heaven's sake,' I said. 'Every time you say "Gamesmaster", I keep thinking he's going to make me put on my shorts and do press-ups. But, yeah, this fantasy could do with a bit of spicing up.'

The Avenger leaned towards us across the map, and we heard his joints creak.

'The hour is late,' he murmured. 'When we meet again, shall it be to play this game of dice for striplings; or to join in mortal combat for the land of my forefathers?' Two points of light glittered in the hood.

'No contest,' I said.

'Mortal combat, definitely,' said Darren.

'Um, definitely,' said Lorin. 'That is, what sort of mortal? I mean, my mum expects me home by ten thirty.'

The Avenger stood up. He secreted the chart, and flung a Tarot card onto the table. On one side was the hanged man; on the other a map marked with a cross.

'Stour,' said Darren. 'Isn't that the new town where they found all those tumuli?'

'I know where it is,' I said. 'It's past all those warehouse places on the Rochester Road. We could bike it.'

'You haven't written the address,' Lorin grumbled, but the Avenger was already swirling

26

down the stairs.

'He didn't even say thank you for the nibbles!' said Darren. I went to the bathroom to get some air freshener.

When Tuesday night rolled round again, we were in two minds about going. After all, our ad was still up at the Workshop, and some game-player might turn up. On the other hand, it's always been my policy to take the dangerous option. Well, what would you do?

Should the Warlords of Penge:
  (a) stay at home to receive warriors?
  (b) valiantly set forth to meet the mighty challenge?

So we got on our bikes and pedalled off, through the arcades, past the B&Q, towards Stour. It was raining, and a bleak wind was furling newspapers round our wheels. I could barely make out the red light wavering on the back of Darren's bike.

'I bet Lorin doesn't come,' I shouted, trying to keep my spirits up, 'the lily-livered knave.' I had my anorak on, but the spray from passing lorries drenched my jeans. I swerved to avoid a mound which probably used to be a dog, and caught up with Darren. On our left, wire netting crisscrossed oil drums and squashed cars; on our right sprawled a jumble of superstores. We laboured up the hill till our stamina points ran low, then freewheeled down the other side towards Green Acres.

It looked marvellous, just like an architect's model, with a thousand little Monopoly houses. I've always fancied being a property developer when I grow up; it's just model-making on a grand scale.

It was lit up like a Christmas tree with those new streetlamps, globes on poles, and we stopped under one to consult the map.

Should we take (a) Oakwood Drive?
  (b) Riverside Close?
  (c) Meadowsweet Crescent?

'The cross is actually just outside the residential area,' Darren pointed out. We heard a yell, and saw Lorin on his bike.

'Hang on, you guys,' he panted. 'I've done the Close and the Crescent. There's no sign of the Avenger.'

The streets were empty as we rode three abreast down Oakwood Drive. Soon the houses had black windows, then none at all, as if the architect's plan was undrawing itself. After a while the house shapes were merely sketched in with trenches. The road, with its lollipop lamps, was losing confidence and trailing away.

Darren stopped. 'This can't be right,' he said. 'I vote forget the whole thing, and go and get a burger somewhere.'

I braked as a ravine gaped before me. 'We've lost the road, or where the road should be,' I said, peering in. Some three metres down I could see the dark shape of my head reflected in rain water. 'This place is one huge building site.'

Time to decide: Should we: (a) go back to town?
  (b) explore the treacherous labyrinth of trenches?

'I'm with Darren,' said Lorin. 'This is getting silly. It could be, I mean, sort of dangerous.'

Put like that there's no choice, as far as I'm concerned.

'You do what you like,' I called over my shoulder. 'I've got an appointment with destiny.' I got off my bike and wheeled it into the muddy waste.

'Come back, you pretentious prat,' Darren shouted. 'You *stupid git*!' I heard him throw down his bike and start to pick his way through the filth.

'Let's go,' pleaded Lorin.

'I can't, the little bastard's my responsibility.'

The trenches at this point were only a metre apart, and kept intersecting. They were leading me to the main construction site, where the land was carved up like a tub of ice cream. I saw rows of pillars supporting nothing, and a vast oblong of raw cement, the foundation for what a sign described as 'Meadowsweet Mall'. I leaned my bike against a pillar and started to climb a pyramid of marble slabs so that I could look round for the Avenger. As I clung to the slippery stack, something clattered downwards to rest by my fingertips. It was a sword.

Raising my eyes, I saw the Avenger at the summit. It had stopped raining, but the sky still boiled, churning his robes like seaweed in the purple night. Below me were Darren and Lorin, their upturned faces childish with the mouths open.

'Pay me heed, Mordred,' the Avenger called. 'This is the land that you and your barbarian forefathers wrested from me and my forefathers. I challenge you, now, to fight for it.'

'That's nothing to do with us!' yelled Darren. 'Who do you think we are, the Department of the

Environment? Leave Dale alone. He's just a kid.'

'Mordred summoned me, and I cannot return till the battle is lost or won,' the monk insisted.

'All right,' I cried, 'I'm not afraid of progress. And I'm not afraid of you. Come down and fight.'

I seized the sword and slipped back. Like lightning streaks, another two swords zipped past me down the pile. I landed on my knees, and as I groped for my sword, I saw that Lorin was already brandishing his. The Avenger stalked towards him. We watched the glitter in the moonlight; then the Avenger made a small shift, and Lorin's sword was gone. The boy backed a few steps and turned towards the houses. Whichever way he ran, the trenches cut him off; it was a maze. The monk followed without haste, his hands folded into his sleeves.

Darren crept up beside me and took my wrist. He was pulling me away.

'We can't leave Lorin,' I said. I tugged my arm free and ran after them. By now, Lorin was backed against a wall. He turned, scrabbling at the bricks, and we saw the Avenger advance; with a gentle, almost fatherly gesture he leaned forwards to embrace the boy. I glimpsed Lorin's face, his throat black-striped by the Avenger's fingers; then he was lost to sight in the swashing robes.

HIS ADVENTURE ENDS HERE.

'Come *on*,' Darren whispered. When I looked again, the Avenger had vanished. So had Lorin. I ran to the spot where they'd been, but there was nothing to see. Just a baseball cap floating deep in the earth.

'For God's sake, Dale,' Darren hissed, 'could you please, for once in your life, do as you are told?'

'I want my bike,' I said, and headed back. My shoes were dragging in the mud, and I pulled them off to run in bare feet. I was panting as I ran, and coughing too, from the tears and snot. When I reached the site of the mall, I saw the Avenger was already on the marble hill at the other side. His hands were raised, fingers enmeshed as though in prayer. The concrete rectangle between us glistened in the moonlight, cold and shiny as an ice rink.

He chuckled, and called across, 'One youth may yet live, if the other is prepared to do battle. Who shall it be? Make your choice.'

What should I have done?
   (a) Fight for my bike, my honour and my brother's life?
   (b) Flee like a paltry coward?

I was angry on Lorin's behalf, and, besides, you know my philosophy. I drew the sword from my belt and set out across the freshly laid cement. Very freshly laid. My feet sank to the ankles. A few more steps, and I could barely pull each foot out again. I was getting into difficulties, for no sooner had I dragged one leg out than the weight on the other pulled me deeper into the morass. It was cold, and felt as if my grave was closing in on me.

'Darren!' I shouted. I had sunk to my waist and could barely turn to look for him. I clawed the surface, twisting my body till I glimpsed his silhouette on a ridge; he was running away. The cement squeezed my ribs as if to wring me out. I flung my head back then, as I drifted downwards, and bellowed.

A shadow scarfed my eyes. It was that of our enemy, who stretched a hand down; I reached to meet it. For a second, his putrefying strands of sinew hugged my warm pink flesh. I shuddered. He let my hand go, and placed both his lightly on my hair, like a blessing. I felt the pressure on my head grow. His foul garments swung about my face as he leaned forward with the weight of his whole body. As I went under, only my fist pierced the surface, still gripping the sword.

Something struck my shins. It was as if God had spooned me from his porridge, for I suddenly found myself in the air. Looking down, I saw Darren in the cab of a mechanical digger. I called out to him, but he was wrestling with the levers, trying to bring the claw that held me back to earth.

It dipped, and I tumbled over the teeth onto the edge of the mall. The digger lurched towards me, but the caterpillar wheels were already half immersed. Darren climbed on top of the cab.

'Crawl along the arm,' I shouted. The digger began to tip, and he sprang clear in a soaring leap. As its huge weight struck the surface, the dinosaur neck writhed, cables twitching; then the engine choked, and the monster became still as the swamp submerged it. I saw our enemy between the caterpillar tracks where it had been, and cried out, but Darren grabbed me.

'It's all right,' he said. 'You're safe now.'

I saw that our foe was rolled out, a long black shape as flat as a gingerbread man. Cement slopped his outline.

'Take my jacket,' Darren said. He put it round my shoulders, rubbing my arms to warm them. I found my shoes, and we got on our bikes. We rode home without speaking.

We were both thinking about Lorin. Silly kids often die on building sites and no one asks questions, but it's so unfair, because I was the silly kid, not Lorin. Not any more, though. I've grown up.

WELL DONE, TRAVELLER! YOU HAVE SUCCEEDED IN YOUR QUEST.

So that was it: no more adventure gaming. On Saturday I went back to the Games Workshop to take down our advert. I scanned the noticeboard. Our ad had gone, but from the same red drawing pin hung a parchment which read:

All ye armies of the undead, from Cambria to Mercia, from Wessex to the Pictish Kingdom, rise up, oh rise up, I command ye! Let legions of darkness go forth in mighty columns – shake the earth from your swords, grind them sharp as viper's fang, and lay waste with bloody slaughter all at:
65 Bexley Avenue, Penge,
8–10 p.m. Tuesday.

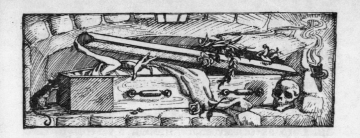

A SKELETON AND HIS BRIDE

The three girls smeared white make-up over each other's faces, then rubbed the black on their cheeks and round their eye sockets.

'It's luminous,' Lynn told Genna and Kelly. 'We'll scare the neighbours witless.' They gibbered at each other in the bathroom mirror, then went to find Lynn's mum.

'Have you got any old sheets?'

'Yep,' was the reply, 'and they're on the beds, so you're not having 'em.'

'We'll bring them back.'

'Oh yeah, all muddied, with holes cut for your faces.'

'God, you're so mean sometimes. How can we go trick-or-treating unless we dress up?'

'There are some old curtains in the spare-room wardrobe. That's my last offer, or I'll be late for the party. Do be good girls. I don't want to hear you've been tying doorhandles together, or squirting water through letter boxes.'

They ran upstairs to the little room at the end of the passage, and clambered over the suitcases, hair dryers and broken fires, which crawl there to die. At the bottom of the wardrobe was a pink candlewick bedspread and some chintz curtains. Holding one against herself, Lynn looked in the wardrobe mirror.

'My mum's such a cow,' she said, 'she never lets me do what I want.'

'It doesn't matter,' said Genna, 'as long as we dress up as something. I'll look for stuff to tart them up with.' She dug around in the cardboard boxes by the bed while Lynn went through the wardrobe.

'How's this?' she asked. Lynn looked round to see Genna cloaked in a curtain, with a toy skunk sitting on her head; it was held there by a belt fastened under her chin, its tail hanging down the back of her head, the nose bobbing perkily on high.

'Weird or what?' she said.

'There's something familiar about the general outline,' Lynn said. 'I know. You look like the widowed Queen Victoria.'

Kelly put on the pink bedspread and a parchment lampshade with galleons painted on it. The two of them looked like a scenario for *The Fly III* – 'Velcome, I am ze mad scientist. But, before you step into ze molecular converter, be *sure* zere is nothing in it – like a fly, or a skunk, or a parchment lampshade with loopy fringes . . .'

'If you think I'm walking down the street looking like that!' Lynn said, and clattered the hangers along the wardrobe rail. Her hand fell on fabric, and as she lifted the hanger, a cloud of silk billowed into the room. She laid it out on the bed.

'Fabulous!' breathed Kelly. 'Are you going to wear it when you get married?'

'Married, me? Never. No, I'm going to wear it

36

tonight.' Lynn pulled off her jeans and sweatshirt and slid into the wedding dress. It felt like moonbeams. She stood before the mirror, eddying cascades of silk around her. Genna reached up and placed the orange-blossom wreath on Lynn's head, then they all looked at her reflection.

It was an old mirror, with glass that rippled the image as if she was under water. Genna broke the awed silence. 'You can't wear that out of doors. It's really old, it must be worth a packet. And the train would get filthy.'

Lynn gazed in the mirror at her bone-white face entwined with tendrils of gold hair, at her shimmering, luminous form; it seemed positively supernatural. Reaching behind for the train, a sweep of honeysuckle lace, she tied it round her neck like a scarf till just a metre drifted down.

'Let's go!' she said.

It was a fine autumn night, misty, but with a breeze. Overhead the trees simmered like chicken vindaloo, spattering saffron leaves along the road. Kelly had a carrier bag.

'We'll share everything out later,' she said. 'We mustn't eat sweets in the dark, in case some nutter's put razor blades in them. They do that in America, you know; I saw it on the six-o'clock show.'

Their street had large houses which tended to be institutions or bedsitters, lived in by people without children. Still, it was fun writing rude messages on the doors. Outside number 56 they ran into the local weirdo, with his floor-length mac and trolley of free newspapers. He greeted the girls like longlost friends.

'May I have the pleasure, madam?' he asked Lynn, and swung her into a waltz. Whirling through the mist, they danced with the leaves.

'I'm spinning round, and the world's spinning with me,' he sang dreamily. 'You have to be mad to live here, but it doesn't help.'

'Sometimes I think I'm the only person round here with any grasp on reality,' said Lynn. 'We've got to go now, but thank you.' The Glossop kids and the Jenningses were coming down the street.

'But I do like a party,' he protested, as they all crowded up the steps to the next house. Lynn rang the bell.

A light went out in the hall, and they heard whispering. The door opened a crack.

'What do you want?'

'Trick or treat!'

The crack widened, and candlelight flickered up the woodwork.

'That'll be a Halloween pumpkin,' Lynn told Genna, who was shivering. 'Too much imagination, that's your trouble.'

A voice oozed through the crack. 'Would you care for a pickled frog? Cockroach candies?'

Genna flew down the steps and along the road. As the others jeered after her, the door swung wide.

There, in the dark hall, stood a skeleton. The skull glowed, white light splintered between its teeth and beamed through the eye holes; the bone seams stood out like wriggles of black thread.

The group screamed and fell down the steps, tumbling over the newspaper trolley.

'Silly girls,' said the weirdo. 'That's the nurses' hostel. Don't you know when you're having your legs pulled?' Sure enough, the doorway was

38

full of nurses.

'Won't you stop for treats?' they teased. 'You can't be scared of our old Jim!' Now the light was on, it was obvious that he was just a medical skeleton hanging on a stand. They'd put a candle in the skull.

Genna's friends ran after her, punching each other and making spooky noises.

'I've had enough,' she said, as they walked along the road. 'Perhaps we should pack it in.'

'You're feeling foolish because you were scared,' Lynn said.

'No,' she replied, with that upward inflexion which shows someone's lying. 'I was bored. You're all so immature. And we're not getting many sweets.'

'Those who wear skunks as hats can hardly accuse other people of immaturity. You're chicken. That's what it comes down to.'

'I am not chicken.'

'Oh yes, you are. Chicken-shit scared. Look, I'll bet you five pounds you can't walk through St Luke's graveyard at midnight. That's when all the spirits come out, you know, the undead, and walk the earth.'

'I do know. And I bet you ten pounds I can. You're sick, Lynn.' She turned to the Glossops. 'D'you know what her favourite poetry is? The "In Memoriams" in the *Herald*.'

'If all the world was ours to give,' Lynn quoted lugubriously,

'We'd give it, yes, and more,
To see the face of dear old Dad
Come smiling through the door . . .'

'See?' said Genna, as Lynn gave a death's-head

39

grin. 'Morbid. I'm going home.'

'. . . We didn't see him close his eyes,' Lynn went on in even gloomier tones, drawing the veil across her face,

'We didn't hear him sigh.
We only heard that he had gone
Without a last goodbye.'

'She even keeps cuttings,' Genna went on. 'It's macabre.'

'Tasteless and insensitive's what I call it,' said Kelly.

The *Catford Herald* was Lynn's favourite newspaper. Not just the obituaries, but the inquests, too. She'd once read a prime example to Genna:

When her husband died, grief-stricken Mrs Pat Corey (75) blew up her house in Briardale Ave. She was placed in Peacehaven Retirement Home, but flung herself from a fourth-floor window. Said Matron Miss J. Falmain, 'I leaned out and saw her hanging off the porch. I called down, "Come now, dear. What did you want to do a silly thing like that for?" But she just groaned.'

All Genna had said was, 'God, how awful!' Lynn despaired of her friends sometimes.

'She just likes being shocking,' Genna was saying now. 'It's a way of showing off. Well, I'm not scared. The bet's on. We'll go home first, then everyone'll meet at the lych gate at midnight. Witnesses, right?'

'Witnesses are fine,' Lynn said, 'but they're staying at the gate, or the bet's off. You're facing those zombies alone.'

She watched her friends walk into the mist, then

wished the weirdo goodnight and made for her house. One stop on the way – the nurses' hostel. This time she didn't ring the bell, but quietly nudged the door open. Jim was just inside, with a nurse's hat on and an umbrella hanging from his clavicle. Lynn took them off and lifted his chain from the hook. The candle still glowed, casting butterflies of light down the steps.

His eggshell skull glowed warmly under her hand as his toes tap-danced along the pavement beside her. She thought how good they must look together: her face silvered by his fiery eyes, her hair streaming, silk leaping round his sharp bones; a well-matched pair. And she was satisfied with the reactions of wanderers returning from the pub – it couldn't be often that they came across a skeleton and his bride out for a walk on a foggy autumn night.

When she got home, Lynn blew out the candle and laid Jim on the carpet. There was no string, but she found a hammer and a bag of nails, which she put in a duvet cover.

When the kitchen clock said eleven thirty, she threw the bag of bones over her shoulder and set off to the church. There was no one about. The lych gate wasn't locked, and she walked into the graveyard. It was a lovely old place, with crumbling angels, family tombs like stone garden sheds, flat graves so mossy you could sleep on them, small graves . . .

'Hannah Elspeth Purley, aged 2 years. Our Darling Baby, gone to the arms of Jesus.' For a while she gave in to the common compulsion to seek one's own name on gravestones, but they were hard to read, not only because it was dark, but also because the carved letters were half erased by time. You'd think if your name was carved on stone, at least that would be immortal.

She slithered on the horse-chestnut leaves and fell headlong between the graves. As she struggled onto her elbows, she had a sudden illusion that the graves were leaning over to watch her. It's a good thing I'm not like Genna, she thought. Imagination doesn't get the better of *me*. She stumbled up and made for the cedar tree, dragging the duvet bag over the long grass.

Gripping it in her teeth, she climbed upwards, one, two, three branches high, clinging to the coarse trunk. Needles scraped her face; the bark was sticky. She chose a horizontal branch and crawled along it, the bones creaking behind her. Then she squatted down and hauled in her skirt.

She groped for the hammer and nails. What with the darkness and the dress blowing everywhere so that her hands were tangled in lace, she lost several nails before one went through his chain. The thud of the hammer shook the tree, and bits of bark and raindrops sprinkled her hair. She lowered the skeleton till he swung free, his globe of a head revolving below her . . . three turns to the left . . . three turns to the right . . .

She crouched down and waited. The tree sighed around her as a breeze cut the mist, and she shivered. To raise her spirits, she proclaimed 'To a late Auntie':

'Oh, you who have an Auntie,
Do cherish her with care.
For you never know when
You'll turn round and look and find that
she's not there.'

When Lynn was younger and less cynical, she'd wondered at the endless columns of verse in the *Herald*. It had impressed her the way the local dead had so many grieving relatives, and she'd found it comforting to think her family would be heartbroken if anything should happen to her. But then she'd heard that the undertakers put pressure on relations because they get a backhander from the *Herald* for each advert.

She didn't see her family falling for a scam like that. They were a hard-nosed lot. When Grandpa died, Lynn's nan had taken the flowers off the coffin and brought them home, because she'd said she needed cheering up more than he did. For a week she'd had 'Sydney' written in pink carnations on the mantelpiece.

Five minutes to twelve, and the wedding dress was clinging to Lynn's cold skin. She was sure Genna wouldn't show. Below her, ivy leaves flicked their sharp tongues. She watched as shadows squirmed through the grass and the moss on the graves began, she could have sworn, to assume a glistening, furry texture; it was crawling, so she closed her eyes and prayed, 'Dear cousin Bill, we love you still, we never knew that you were ill . . .' but when she reopened them the horrors were still there, radiating until the whole graveyard became one beast, its humps and hollows undulating as it breathed.

'Well,' came a voice, 'if it was me, I'd rather pay up.'

Lynn's heart slowed. All was normal again; her fears scurried back in their holes.

'Yeah, but ten pounds!' she heard Genna answer. 'Besides, I've got my pride. I can't let Lynn get one up on me.'

Someone else, possibly Jago Jennings, said, 'Anyway, I see she hasn't turned up! Who's the most chicken of all?'

Lynn had been ready to climb down, ready, in fact, to run over and hug them, but at that she curled up tightly and crouched there, holding the chain.

The gate squeaked. Footsteps hesitantly tapped across the flagstones, and through a gap in the branches she saw the curve of Genna's head. Lynn reached down for the skeleton's chain and tugged it.

'Oooooaaah!' she moaned, and 'Nooooooo. Eeeeeeeeeh!' The skeleton swayed, his ankles clattering, and Lynn crammed a wrist into her mouth to stop a fit of the giggles. The steps below paused. There was a shriek, and through the gap she glimpsed a hand, a flap of skirt, a flying calf and foot; there was a torrent of footsteps to the gate, which banged shut.

'I saw a ghost! I did! Under the big tree!'

The voices mocked. 'Oh yeah? Can't fool us!'

'Go and see for yourselves, then. I'd rather pay Lynn fifty pounds than go in there.'

'You go, Jago.'

'Not me!'

'Nor me!'

There was some scuffling, then the gate crashed shut again and the chatter melted away down the road.

That crash sounded as final as the closing of a tomb lid. Lynn wiped her nose on her sleeve. Now I know what jokes are for, she thought, and having a laugh, sending up, the stuff I do all the time. It's papering over the cracks to stop the fear getting out.

Mist folded round her then, tucking her in, and suddenly she felt like a dying person feels when the sounds of life finally shrink, and darkness fills his eyes and ears and mouth. All the cold loneliness in the world festered in that churchyard. The graves, with their little peaked roofs, seemed like porches, doorways to hell; and that hell not fiery, but a place of dragging weariness, where bodies which can no longer keep up with life are overtaken by decay. Lynn could no longer deny it; she was terrified.

The church clock began to strike. She counted each reverberating beat, knowing that twelve o'clock on the thirty-first of October is the time for eyeless horrors to wake from hibernation and squeeze through their cracked sepulchres, slither from under their stones, for the annual outing.

In the pine needles, something fluttered. Oh, God! thought Lynn. It might be just a crow. She edged along the branch. She wouldn't look back – what you can't see, can't scare you. She considered getting the hammer, but there didn't seem much point in attacking something already dead. Reaching the trunk she clung to it, swinging her legs over, but as she swivelled she glimpsed something twitch from the corner of her eye. She refused to look. She climbed down another branch and felt a touch, soft as a feather, on her neck. Slowly she turned. She saw it then, transparent, thin, a long white arm floating on darkness, a diaphanous membrane swooping towards and around her throat. I'm not imagining this ... she thought.

Something gripped her throat, squeezing it tighter and tighter, throttling her, until waves broke, stars exploded in her brain, and she had no choice but to jump . . .

From the *Catford Herald and Post*, 2 November 1994:

BIZARRE MURDER

Yesterday schoolgirl Lynn Frazer (14) was found hanging from the cedar tree in St Luke's churchyard. She wore a wedding dress and had been strangled by the train, which was nailed to a branch. A skeleton entangled with the body was suspended from the same nail. Satanic ritual is suspected. See: In Memoriam, p. 32.

FRENCH RESISTANCE

'This is a friendly school, Stephen,' he said. 'A real home from home. And we're all terribly informal. You mustn't call me "sir".'

'What's your name, then; Joe, or Bill, or what?' Stephen asked. There was a jagged intake of breath across the class.

'Mr Manners, boy. You must call me Mr Manners.' He coughed. 'Well,' he went on briskly, 'say goodbye to your father. Don't worry, Mr Cole. We'll put backbone in the lad. "Manners maketh man", as I like to jest.'

'I can't thank you enough for taking Stephen at such short notice. This army life, I'm afraid . . . so unpredictable.' The man hugged his son. 'Goodbye, then,' he said.

The boy stared at the door as it closed.

'Well, there's work to be done, Cole. Give out the French books. Come now, we don't want to be a big crybaby, do we?'

Stephen blinked, his white face flushing pink round the eyes and nose. As he reached for the books, a jug of pencils crashed to the floor. I relaxed.

Here he is, I thought. This year's scapegoat.

Every day there'd be something, usually about Cole's untidiness. (I think Mr Manners has got this thing about order to make up for his own middle-aged decay – he's got a head like a ham in collar and tie.)

'Cole, why are your socks at half-mast?'

'What, Mr Manners?'

'*Pardon*, Mr Manners. So you're deaf as well as slovenly! In the corner, if you please. In the waste-paper bin. The "sin bin", as I have humorously deemed it. No, both feet, Cole. Don't start mizzling again. Husayn, kindly conjugate for us the present subjunctive of *être*.'

After half an hour, he said, 'My dear Cole, I'd completely forgotten you! Let me see; we'll play a little game. I do realise French can be rather dry, so we'll have some fun, eh? Well, now. Let's pretend your father, who we know is fighting for Queen and country on foreign soil, let's pretend he's standing in front of an enemy firing squad. Now, Cole, the captain of the firing squad says to you, "Little boy, I shall spare your father's life if you do one small thing for me. Just put *mourir* in the future tense." That is, of course, an -*ir* verb, meaning "to die". Can you do that one tiny thing, Cole? Remember, your father's life depends on you.'

I've noticed Cole's got a lot thinner over the weeks, that's why his socks are always drooping. There are marks like lavender thumbprints under each eye, and his skin's gone quite transparent.

'*Je meure*,' he began, '*tu* – '

Mr Manners clicked his tongue. 'Dear, oh dear, what a pity. We'll have to put the blindfold on. Out of the bin, Cole. Now invert it over your head. That's right, pull it down.'

The class tittered. We know what's expected of us.

'This is a good opportunity to do the imperative, as in "Die!"' Mr Manners went on, and he explained it for several minutes. Then he said, 'Have you got that, Cole?'

'I can't see the blackboard, sir, because the bin's over my head.'

'That's a shame, because this is your last chance. The imperative of *mourir*. At once, please. The firing squad are raising their rifles. They're all pointing at your father. The drums are rolling. They're pulling back the safety catches. Five ... four ... three ... two ...'

'*Je mourais*,' Cole whimpered.

'*One!*' roared Mr Manners, and, grasping his metal ruler, crashed it repeatedly on the bin. 'Wrong, wrong, *wrong*, you STUPID boy.' The bin tolled a final reverberating clang as Cole, clutching the rim, stumbled to his knees.

I know what you're thinking, but let me tell you, there's no room for compassion in public school. It's like being taken into care without the care, it's a refugee bunkhouse for the stateless, the difficult, the dispossessed; it's every man for himself.

A few weeks later, I tried to borrow a pen during French.

'Who's talking?' boomed Mr Manners. We looked at Cole. Mr Manners stood up. He lifted his chair and swung it round beside his desk. Then he sat down again.

'Here, Cole,' he called pleasantly. Cole walked

slowly to the front of the class.

'Kneel down,' said Mr Manners, 'and look at me. Don't avert your face in that sneaky way; look me in the eye, like a man.' He wrenched Cole's chin till their faces were an inch apart. Cole shut his eyes against the spraying saliva. '*Look* at me, I tell you! Your soul has no secrets from me. I can detect the arrogance in that sulky little face. Who do you think you are, anyway, eh? Eh? Better than the rest of us, *heh*?'

Mr Manners always starts in a whisper and builds to a shout in a gradual crescendo as the blood darkens and swells his face.

'How grieved your father would be, if he knew your true character. That loving father, who spends all his money to get this *worth*less, *wick*ed, *thank*less child an education! A little education in humility is what you need. Bow your head, boy.'

He clapped his knees together with Cole's head jammed between them. As the boy's face pointed to the floor, so his bottom rose.

We laughed politely.

'What jolly little boys you are, to be sure!' exclaimed Mr Manners. 'I fear young Cole here has no sense of humour. This is a happy school, you dismal sprog; so we shall conjugate *rire*, which means "to laugh".'

As we chanted, Mr Manners kept time with his flat palms on Cole's head. '*Nous rions* (whack), *vous riez* (whack).' So well trained are we that we kept going even when we noticed Cole was up to something. From my desk at the end of the row, I had a good view. I could see his bony fingers tugging, ever, ever so gently, at the laces of Mr Manners's shoes. I suppose he'd been staring at them so long, he couldn't help himself. It was mesmerising, as we worked our way through the pluperfect, watching Cole undo them. During the imperfect he tied a knot at the end of each and unthreaded them through the holes until they were long enough to meet in the middle. By the end of the past historic, he'd knotted them together.

The bell rang. 'Off you go, Cole. Well done, boys. No unseemly scramble, for once!' Mr Manners stood up and put the register in the desk drawer. He gathered his books and put his pen in his pocket. He blew his nose, watching us over the handkerchief. He straightened his tie. And then, with a puzzled expression, he started to walk off.

'Timber!' cried Cole, his face racked with joy and terror. Thirty desk lids rattled as Mr Manners struck the floor. Painfully, he rolled over and sat up. His hands dabbed around until he found his glasses – one lens webbed with cracks – and put them on. No one laughed.

Cole flattened himself against the wall, legs bent, fingers outstretched, like a chalk diagram showing the position of a murder victim, as Mr Manners fumbled with his laces. Unable to untangle the knot, he gave a vicious tug which snapped them. He put a hand on the desk and hauled himself upright, then limped up to Cole. His untidy features hung over Cole's small neat face: the eyeballs were held back by walnut-shell skin, the flobby lips, sprouting from cheeks like salami, bulged down and wobbled as he spoke.

'You wretched little toad!' he spat. 'If I had my way . . . never mind. Kingsley, would you kindly lock him in the stationery cupboard.'

Cole started biting his nails.

'Oh, please, sir, not again. You know I can't go in small spaces, it makes me panicky. I'm really sorry, sir.'

'One of the many problems besetting education today is the banning of corporal punishment. Incarceration, if only for an hour or two, is the best we can offer. Kingsley, if you please . . .'

I took Cole downstairs, past the laundry, past the boiler room, to the stationery cupboard.

'It's horrible down here. Don't lock me in, Kingsley, I can't bear it. Why don't I just hide in the shrubbery?'

'Because he'll find out when he comes to unlock you.' I was sorry for him; after what he'd done he deserved a break. 'Tell you what,' I said, 'I'll give you my Mars bar. It's not that bad in here, there's a light. I hide here myself sometimes, when it's football.'

He sat in a corner of the cupboard and, drawing up his knees, began to pick at the scabs. Black eyes gazed up at me from puddled sockets.

'Snug, isn't it?' I said. 'Nice and warm, next to the boiler.' To my embarrassment, a tear slid down his cheek, so I quickly shut the door and locked it. Doesn't know when he's well off, I thought. Mars bar instead of semolina.

We had cross-country running that afternoon, then it was half-term, so I didn't see Cole for a while.

We got back on Sunday night, and unpacked.

'Where's the hero?' I asked.

'He's back,' said Matsuda. 'I saw his suitcase downstairs.'

'Hardly anyone else is,' Mahfouz said. 'They've

all got flu.'

After lights out we crept down to the tuck room. It's traditional, we always have a midnight feast to cheer ourselves up on the first night back. Nakaoka and Husni from Saxon House were there, and Husayn and Mbulu, who are Normans, and I think Patel, who's a Celt, was there too. They'd brought a good selection of sweets, which we spread across the windowsill between us, then sat there, swinging our legs. Outside, the wind was ruffling silver patterns over the lawn, wetly stirring the bushes. The windows were black in the Old Building opposite, its medieval spires clawing the wild sky. There was no sound but that of the wind, and of our sucking.

'What's that?' I whispered. Something had moved by the chapel. We watched a shape, half hidden by the elms, advance up the drive. Shifting, formless, it flickered through the slits of space between the trees. At length it stepped onto the lawn and began to walk across. We saw then that it was a figure in a belted robe and a helmet, like those worn in the Crusades. Through the wet glass, the luminous shape dissolved as it passed, till we could track it only by the gleam of the helmet.

Matsuda tumbled off the windowsill and crouched so that he could just see over the top. He was gripping my leg, his nails digging through my pyjama trousers. As the apparition glided over the lawn, Mahfouz started to scream, and I clamped my palm over his mouth.

'Shut up!' I hissed. All I wanted to do was to run back to bed and put my head under the covers, but I waited till he was quiet, then leaned across the sill and wiped our breath from the window with my sleeve. My heart was tumbling in my chest. I stared down. Then, as the moon slipped through the clouds, I began to laugh weakly.

'Look – ' I pointed – 'it's not a ghost at all, it's Cole up to his tricks again!'

First I'd recognised the blue dressing gown with the striped piping on the collar, and the cord all frayed where he chews it; after that, I could see that the helmet was obviously the French-room waste bin.

Well, that was it, for us. Cole became instant legend. For the next few days he wasn't in class, didn't even come to meals, but occasionally could be sighted flitting across a landing or, at dusk, slinking like a phantom through the dormitory.

'He's gone underground,' I said. 'It's just like the French Resistance.'

'We've got our own freedom fighter,' Matsuda agreed proudly.

It was on the Wednesday that we ran out of rough paper.

'Kingsley, my young Mercury,' called Mr Manners, 'be so good as to fly to the supplies cupboard and procure us some.'

Cole was right about the basement. It's not very pleasant. When you open the door, silverfish and cockroaches scurry under the washing machines. The one bulb hanging from the concrete ceiling swings in the draught, sending monumental shadows rearing up behind the freezers. You can't hear yourself think, what with the boiler roaring away and all the machines going. There's the most god-awful stink, too. I noticed it as I hurried along the passage. I unlocked the cupboard door.

The first thing I saw was the mess. Several shelves were down, tipping pink and yellow and blue exercise books across the floor. Cole was crouched in the corner, almost hidden by an avalanche of torn paper.

'So this is where you've been hiding out!' I exclaimed.

He didn't say anything. I peered closer. He really did look dreadful, worse than I'd ever seen him; his skin was shiny taut over the sharp framework of bone, with scoops of shadow under his cheekbones. A blue stain mapped his lips and chin.

'I've heard of glue-sniffing,' I said, 'but ink-drinking's a new one on me.' I leaned over and gave him a tickle. 'Come on, wake up!'

He swayed towards me, then clumsily subsided over the books and ink bottles. His lips dropped open, revealing Prussian blue teeth. I faltered. Then I ran like hell.

'Excuse me, Mr Manners,' I said, from the classroom doorway.

'What is it, Kingsley? We are awaiting our rough paper.'

'Please, Mr Manners . . .'

He saw my face, and came to the door.

'It's Cole, sir,' I said. We started to walk down the corridor, faster and faster. I broke into a run, and I heard his feet thundering behind me. Down the stairs, through the laundry, past the boiler room . . . We stood at the open door of the stationery cupboard.

Mr Manners pushed his knuckles into his mouth. He leaned against the door and closed his eyes, then opened them a crack to squint sideways at poor Cole.

'Oh, my God!' he croaked. 'I forgot. I clean forgot.' He bent an arm against the doorframe and banged his head repeatedly against it. Then he straightened up and took a deep breath.

'Look here, Kingsley; the poor little chap is clearly a victim of the flu epidemic. You must help me get him tucked up in bed, and I will telephone his father.'

I took his ankles, while Mr Manners held the body under the armpits. It was surprisingly light, and apart from some difficulty with doors, we moved him along fairly fast.

'Thank heaven the undertaker is a mason,' grunted Mr Manners.

'Please, sir,' I said, 'I can't stand the way his hands keep banging on the stairs. Couldn't we put them in his pockets?'

'Shh, Kingsley, no time for that. Quick, quick. Nearly there. Good. On the bed, gently now. Get his shoes off. Right. Tell the class to learn "In the Patisserie". I'll be down in a tick when I've cleaned him up.'

'All right, sir.'

'And don't forget to wash your hands.'

'No, sir.'

'And Kingsley . . .'

'Yes, sir?'

'I can rely on you, Kingsley? I mean, your parents were so proud of you winning the scholarship, and, of course, we couldn't pay out that sort of money unless you were a dependable member of our little community. Are you with me?'

'Yes, sir, but . . .' This was bothering me. 'I saw Cole yesterday, and he was fine.'

'Ye gods!' He laughed hysterically. 'Just look at

57

the state of him, Kingsley! Go on, get out, get out.'

On a beautiful October afternoon, the school held a memorial service in the chapel. Those of us who are in the choir put on our red surplices and filed into the pews along the aisle. Behind us stood the staff and the rest of the school, and behind them, the parents. Sunshine sliced through the stone arches, gilding our hymnals, bleaching the candle flames. The organ played. Gazing beyond it, I saw the glitter of tears in many a parent's eye. Then my voice rose with the others: 'Yea, though I walk through the valley of the shadow of death . . .' The psalm swelled until its pure notes spun about the pillars, soaring upwards through the lines of light.

As the echoes faded, Mr Manners shuffled some papers and rose to his feet. He strode down the aisle, footsteps ringing, black robe ballooning behind him, and mounted the spiral stairs to the pulpit. It's a tall pulpit, and he looked imposing as he spread his notes across the carved eagle. Taking a handkerchief from his pocket, he wiped his eyes. Then he replaced it, put on his new glasses and, grasping the eagle on each wing, leaned forwards.

'On this sad day,' he began, 'we join together in prayer for the soul of a gentle child who, having enriched our lives, is no longer with us. "Suffer little children to come unto me," said the Lord, and Stephen Cole, a boy of such immense promise . . .'

I don't think he realised he was losing the attention of the congregation; for, one by one, we were transfixed by the sight of his brogues. These were planted firmly on each side of the lectern, so beautifully polished that a ray of sun lent their chestnut toes an almost transcendental glow. The laces had black metal tips which glinted as slowly, slowly, first on the right foot, then on the left, they unthreaded themselves. Invisible hands knotted the ends, and then, with infinite care, tied them in a bow in the middle.

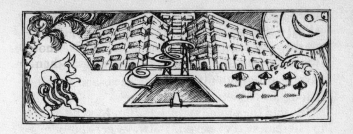

THE PIGGYWIG CLUB

Playleader Suzie Barker.

SATURDAY

a.m. Scavenger Hunt, Drawing Competition.

p.m. Junior Disco. Do the Funky Chicken with Percy the Piggywig!

'How *dare* you say Paul can't join!' the woman exclaimed. 'The only reason we booked this holiday was for the club. We're on the scuba-diving course, you see. There'd be no one to keep an eye on him.'

'I do see the problem,' the playleader apologised. 'It's just that the age range is supposed to be three to eleven, and he's thirteen. Normally it wouldn't matter, but this week I'm afraid the kids are half his age, or less.'

'Well, that's not our fault, is it? Thousands of pounds, this holiday cost us.'

'Yes, well, OK. Fine. I'm sure it'll be all right, really. We'll have loads of fun, won't we, Paul? Would you like to join the others? We're doing some colouring-in.'

Paul looked at the circle of nineteen dwarfish

faces in the rear of the table-tennis hut.

'That's right, darling,' said his mother. 'Mind you have a terrific time, now.'

He walked over and sat on the single empty stool, resting his chin on his knees, and draping his long arms round his long shins.

'Hi!' said the child on his left. 'I'm Meredith, and I'm the eldest. I'm seven. I always get the orange squash and take the little ones to the toilet.'

'Hi,' said Paul.

'Would you sign this for me?' The boy passed him a booklet, on which was printed: 'Piggywig Friends I made on Holiday'.

Paul flicked through pages of names and addresses while Meredith smiled proudly, his sun-burned cheeks rising as shiny as tomatoes.

'How can these be your friends?' asked Paul. 'None of the kids here can even read or write. Do you just walk up to people like me – total strangers?'

'Are you going to sign it, or what?' Meredith demanded.

Under the address of a Mrs Edith Philpott of Broadstairs, Paul wrote: 'L. E. Fant, 15 Big Drop-pings, Dunghill.'

The boy reached for the book and looked at it. His face squeezed tight.

'Just because I'm seven,' he said, 'doesn't mean I'm stupid. You've spoiled the whole thing. I was going to take it home to show my granny!'

'Glad to see you've made a pal already,' said Suzie.

Meredith ignored her. 'It's *you* who's stupid. In the Piggywig Club when you're thirteen.'

'Perhaps Paul will be my right-hand man, now,'

the playleader said, beaming, 'and get our juice and biscuits. You'll find a tray all ready at the pool bar, OK? And we'll get started on "Mr Biff the Boxer".'

Paul stepped out into the sunshine. In the hut the circle of small children closed round their leader; from the gloom just one pair of eyes, round as ping-pong balls, watched as he trudged through the sandpit.

SUNDAY

Sorry, kids! Suzie's on Airport duty. No club today.

MONDAY

a.m. The Chocolate Game.

p.m. Karaoke night. Do a duet with Percy the Piggywig!

'Quiet, boys and girls. Let's have a bit of hush. *Quiet!* Paul, could you help me pin their numbers on? Right, stand on your stools. When I blow the whistle – I said *when* I blow the whistle, Vanessa – we'll start.'

Slabs of chocolate lolled on white plastic plates; the colour of a really good tan, they bulged, melting at the edges. Already the ants were legging it across the table, breasting the plate rims, and Paul's stomach lurched. On their stools stood the nine-teen children, spoons clutched above their heads, like the audition for an infant remake of *Psycho*.

'OK, Paul, give us the numbers.'

'But I always throw the dice!' cried Meredith.

'*Quiet*, everyone. *Stool*, Meredith, there's a good boy.' Suzie blew the whistle, Paul rattled the dice. 'Five!'

There was a vicious scramble, and several children who'd been knocked down began to cry.

'Three!' he shouted, having difficulty making himself heard.

'Lisa, Lisa,' Suzie was yelling, 'don't wipe your hands in your hair. You'd better go and wash. Paul, would you . . .?'

Meredith grabbed Lisa's arm. 'It's *my* turn to take her,' he said.

The table keeled over, and as the children dived to scrape the chocolate from the floorboards, Paul pulled his stool into a quiet corner. From further down the hut came the peaceful 'tock, tock . . .' of table tennis, mixed with companionable swearing. That was where he should be; with the lads. A ball ricocheted off one of the tables to skitter under the stacked sunbeds. Paul peered underneath and saw what appeared to be swathes of black lace. As his fingers closed on the ball, he realised he was touching spiderwebs patterned by the legs and bodies of a thousand dead ants.

'Thanks,' the lads called, as he tossed it back. 'You all right, then? Like it, do you, in the club? All them organised games?'

He nodded sombrely and looked away, too proud to want to know if they were sorry for him or sniggering.

'Yoohoo!' Suzie called. 'Lisa's back, but we seem to have mislaid Meredith . . .'

Paul got up and walked out to the pool. Dazzled by the sun, he put a hand over his eyes to scan the milling black silhouettes. Three fat fathers sitting on table mats hurtled past him on the water slide.

'Looking for someone?' said a voice behind him. There was a shove in the small of his back, and suddenly solid heat turned liquid, flooded his mouth, his nose, ballooning his pockets in an

64

explosion of bubbles as he fought his way to the surface. As his head shot into the air, he snorted and shook his head, paddling.

On the side, Meredith was giggling behind his hand. Several splashed sunbathers towelled themselves indignantly, and the table-tennis lads came out to see what was going on. One pointed to a notice on the wall. He wagged his finger and, in a voice of oriental wisdom, read out:

'Take notice of lifeguard.
Have fun, but not
at the expense of others.
Extend yourself within endurance.'

Paul swam through the laughter and pulled himself up the ladder to the poolside. Meredith was making for the safety of the hut, and was already halfway across the mini-golf course. Paul loped after him, grabbing a golf club on the way. As Meredith crossed the sandpit, Paul began to sprint. He caught the back of Meredith's shorts and, gathering him up, laid him across the seesaw. Placing a foot on the child's back, he raised the club, and with an immaculate swing struck him hard on the bottom.

TUESDAY
a.m. Sandcastle Competition.
p.m. Bar-B-Que. Do the Locomotion with Percy the Piggywig!

'OK, line up everyone. Find a partner. Paul, if you go in front with Vanessa . . . Have you all got your buckets and spades? All together now: "We're all going on a. . . summer holiday . . ."'

The good thing about leading the procession, thought Paul, was that they couldn't see he wasn't singing.

As he walked, someone behind kept stamping on his flip-flops.

'I'll bet that's you, Meredith,' he said, keeping his temper. 'Do lead, if it's so important to you.'

Meredith directed the children through the village with Vanessa's hand tightly in his. People smiled as she toddled along in her spotted bonnet, conducted with such comical care by a child not much older than herself, who shouted 'Stop!' at every crossing, and 'Flat against the wall, Club!' whenever a car passed.

They found a deserted stretch among the rocks at the end of the beach.

'Let's see some lovely sandcastles,' said the play-leader, sitting down and stretching out her legs.

'I'll look after the club,' said Meredith. 'You have a nice little rest.' He walked up to Paul. 'Do you want to share my beach set?' He held up a bucket with two spades (one large, one small), a rake and a tortoise shape. 'I'm sorry I was nasty. We're the eldest, we should be a team. And I've got this excellent plan.'

'What?'

'We'll dig to Australia. Over there, behind the rock, where it's damp.'

'Wouldn't it be New Zealand?' said Paul. 'We're in Portugal now.'

But as the pit grew, Paul found he was actually enjoying himself. It was surprising how fast the work went with twenty spades. While the sun crawled up the sky, they excavated a deep scoop of beach, shadowed by its own sand heap.

'Too hot,' Paul panted. 'Let's turn it into a

'It would be more fun,' Meredith suggeste
you get in, like my dad does, so we can bury yo

Indulgently, Paul climbed down. He lay back and closed his eyes as the warm spadefuls sprinkled his body. Kids are quite decent, really, he thought. You just have to respect their need for dignity, for responsibility. Perhaps I'll be a teacher one day.

'I'll be Gulliver,' he said, 'like in the cartoon. And you can be the little people who tie me down.' They laughed, patting the sand smooth round his neck.

'You do look funny, just your head sticking out!'

'Not too hard, you guys!' Paul exclaimed as they jumped on the sand to pack it firm. 'I can't move a millimetre.'

'Final touch,' said Meredith, and untied Vanessa's sun bonnet.

'You wouldn't!' Paul wailed, and the children laughed louder as Meredith perched it on top of Paul's protruding head, tying the pink ribbons in a bow under his chin.

'Actually, that's enough, now, Meredith. Joke's over.' He didn't like looking a fool, and was beginning to wonder if he should have trusted the little horror.

'Don't worry. I won't make you wear it.' Meredith rolled the bonnet down over Paul's face so the bow was at the back of his head. Then, with methodical thoroughness, he started stuffing the fabric into Paul's mouth, poking it between his teeth.

Paul was furious. He crunched his jaws shut on Meredith's forefinger; the boy snatched it out and sucked it. His expression didn't change. Paul wriggled his shoulders – he'd had enough – but he was fixed as firmly as if in concrete. Meredith picked up his rake and used the handle to tuck the last stray frills into Paul's mouth.

'We're going to play the marmalade game now,' Meredith told the club. 'It's much more fun than the chocolate game.' He took a carrier bag from his bucket and handed each child a little plastic carton and knife. 'I nicked these from the hotel this morning,' he said. 'Don't tell. What you've all got to do is spread the marmalade over the Sacrifice.'

'But there's only his head!'

'Do a really good job, then. Over the ears, in the hair. Up his nose.'

Behind the rocks, Suzie's closed eyelids flickered at the sound of laughter, and she smiled. She could hear them singing 'Ring-a-Ring-o'-Roses', hear the slap of naked dancing feet.

'What do we do now, Meredith?' she heard them cry.

'Oh, the real fun starts soon. But we can't stay to watch it. It's orange-squash time. Let's climb up the rocks and jump down the other side.'

Behind the rocks, Paul heard the flump of thirty-eight small feet landing on sand. He heard:

'Oh! My gosh, is that the time? I must have dozed off for a tick. OK, everybody, find a partner. Are we all ready? Where's Paul?'

'His mum came,' Meredith's voice answered. 'Took him to lunch.'

'Oh, I don't think so. Parents are always supposed to tell me when they collect a child.'

'Perhaps she was being tactful. I mean, you were asleep, weren't you?'

'Right, well, er, fine, then. Buckets and spades,

and away we go. Let's try the conga to the song of the seven dwarfs.'

Paul cried out, but all that came was a muffled burr. 'With a bucket and spade and a lemonade, yoho,' faded into the distance. He rubbed his cheek frantically along the sand, back and forth, scraping his skin on shards of stone. The ribbon snapped, and he spat out the bonnet. His mouth was dry.

'Suzie!' he croaked. He wrenched his shoulders again, and looked around. Not a soul about. Behind him the sea whispered, while ahead, beyond the rocks, towels flapped – shrunk by distance to a United Nations of green and yellow stripes, red splodges with blue dots, squares of peppermint and mauve.

Above them the sky stretched taut between cliffs, the clenched sun squeezing heat onto his bare head. He'd give anything, now, for a Piggywig hat. Even a bonnet. He tried to think of some Portuguese words, so he could shout for help. *Obrigado*, he remembered, meant 'thank you'.

It must be getting on for one o'clock. Siesta time. No wonder the sun was boring a hole in his skull. No wonder there was no one about.

'Help,' he whimpered, and, gathering all his strength, roared it out. '*Help!*'

The marmalade, which had at least been pleasantly cool, was drying to itchy patches.

That was when he noticed the black line wavering over the rocks. He squinted into the brightness as wispily, like a thread of cotton, the line dribbled onto the sand. It was coming towards him.

Oh, God, he thought. So that's Meredith's little game.

The line split, plaiting and weaving, as the ants

made towards him; they were on the marmalade trail, about five metres away.

The previous night Paul had been woken by a moped, and had shuffled into the villa kitchen for a drink; flicking on the light, he'd seen a similar stripe of ants from the waste bin to the kitchen door, a whole army bearing off a slice of salami. He'd admired the teamwork, the purpose behind the apparently random milling. But how, he wondered now, do they tell live meat from dead? Do they think something fleshy is meat if it doesn't run away? Like a head, for instance?

As they grew closer he found himself staring at the intricate detail of the leader; it was twinned with a shadow as black as itself, so that two sets of eager antennae bobbed across the sand, two thoraxes, a double pointed abdomen, twelve delicate angled legs hurried to lunch. He closed his eyes and again pushed upwards with his feet. Nothing moved.

He looked back. The ants were a metre away. Sweat filmed his eyes and, as he blinked, dry sand sifted through his eyelashes in dust crescents on his sticky cheekbones.

They were so close now, he was looking into each stemmed eye. Each dot and comma of them, every dash and semicolon, as if all the letters in all the words in all the horror stories in the world had escaped, and danced their horrid punctuation towards his throat.

He felt the first tickle, so fine it might have been his imagination, on his Adam's apple. Then another, under his chin. His skin pricked a centimetre below his mouth. There was no doubt about it now, they were swarming on the crease of skin

at the left of his mouth. He started to scream, but a soft hair's touch fluttered round his bottom lip, mapping its curve. Paul snapped his mouth shut and felt a squirming pip between his lips. He didn't dare spit for fear more would wriggle through the pursed gap. Then they were all over his mouth, as high as a moustache. If he closed one eye and peered down, he could just make out the black, curdling horizon of his upper lip. A formation broke away to curl round his right nostril, trekking up the slope beside his nose to the marmalade valley of his eye socket.

Just then – in a blessed relief neither he nor Meredith had anticipated – he felt a cool swirl round his neck. An ant-freckled eddy of sea water swished past him, looping through the shingle. There was a sighing hiss as the wave retreated. Foam flecks streaked the beach, where ants struggled, their upturned legs shuddering. Another wave broke against the back of his head, sweeping round his face, higher this time, to wash away his torture.

The tide was coming in.

MERRYANDREW, MOLE AND SPOON

They built the new supermarket bang on top of the hill, at the crossroads. Joanna, cycling up (slowly, because of her asthma), and seeing the rooks huddled on its post-modern gables, always had the impression of a castle. At first she'd loved it for the space, the hygiene, the sheer crazy abundance of things to buy – a hundred different brands of shampoo, for instance – but after a few weeks, she came to realise that more products means further to push a wayward trolley; and besides, who needs kumquats or Norwegian goat's cheese?

As she struggled round on Friday after school, she considered dumping her trolley and nicking an unattended one in the checkout queue. It would not be shoplifting if she went on to pay for the food, and it would give her a full trolley without the hassle of filling it – a magical mystery trolley, full of things she wouldn't normally eat.

Tortellini, tagliatelle, *Paglia e Fieno*. Quark. Round the bend to Boneless Loins. Then, purple in frosty plastic: liver, kidneys, cured ox tongue. Glad I didn't see it when it was sick, she was thinking, when she noticed the three men.

Wildly out of place they looked, as they shuffled past in saggy coats, hair as matted as Weetabix. Their fingers left greasy snail tracks along the surgically clean cabinets, but what really caught Joanna's attention was that one of them, instead of a trolley, was pushing a large wooden wheelbarrow. He was looking about surreptitiously, while the other two leaned into the frozen-chicken compartment.

She stopped, wondering what to do. Should she get an assistant? But, great heavens, a wheelbarrow! How on earth did they expect to get away with it? She had decided it was none of her business and was reaching for some stuffing, when out of the corner of her eye, she saw a bulky shape being dragged out of the freezer and manhandled into the barrow. Overcome with curiosity, she turned, and saw a woman. Her legs dangled over the back of the barrow, her head hung over the front; the face, upside down, confronted Joanna with a grimace. Her skin was blue, the eyelids closed.

'Can I help?' Joanna cried, running up. 'God, how dreadful! I'll get an ambulance. Did anyone see how she came to fall into the freezer?'

The short man with the hat was busy tucking her arms into the barrow, while the fat one with no teeth tried to bend the legs up; they kept springing out again. The tall man was covering the woman with sacks.

'You can't do that!' Joanna exclaimed. 'I do know you shouldn't move an accident victim. We must get a proper stretcher, and a blanket. I'll fetch the manager at once.'

'Eh, lass,' the big man said, 'doan' ee trouble thysen. We'll get un down t'Infirmary.'

74

'You mean St George's? I know they've got a casualty department. Just wait a sec.'

She ran past Mince and Bacon to a door with a striped mirror window, and banged on it. Kitchen foil, she was thinking, we must wrap her in it till the ambulance comes.

A man in a brown overall put his head round the door. 'There's been an accident,' she cried, breathlessly. 'Look, over there. A lady fell into the . . .' Her voice tailed away. At the other end of the aisle the automatic doors slid back, and against the bright car park she saw the outline of the men and their wheelbarrow. They were scuttling out of sight down the hill.

'Sorry to have bothered you,' she said to the manager. 'They seem to have gone.'

'I'll bet it was those damn tinkers again,' he said. 'Drunk, probably. We caught one little rascal last week, can't have been a day over eight; had a giant packet of Wotsits stuffed up his jumper, and when we followed him, would you credit it, we found the dad waiting in a taxi; biscuits, tinned peas, all sorts stacked on the floor.'

'Oh, well,' Joanna said. 'I expect you're right. Anyway, they said they'd take her to hospital.' The stress was getting to her, and she took a puff at her inhaler. Reclaiming her trolley, she remembered that the woman hadn't looked any cleaner than her rescuers, and avoided the free-range section.

The following week shopping took longer than usual, as her parents were having a barbecue on the Saturday. They both worked, and it was Joanna who usually ended up with the shopping list. She was just delving among the sausages, when she heard the creak rattle, creak rattle, of the wheel-barrow coming down the aisle. Not surprising, really, she thought. You tend to see the same people every week. She dropped a pack of Herbal Cumber-lands into the trolley.

'Hello,' she said. 'How's that lady? All right now?'

The big man grinned, a blurred, wobbly spread of lip. A waft of his breath reached her.

'Aye,' he said. 'She's spick and span. The doctor were right pleased we brought un in.' He scratched his belly. 'Eh, goodly place, this, ain't it? Fine, fresh merchandise. We comes regular.'

'Me too,' said Joanna. 'Well, must be getting on.' She was wondering how to get past them, as the barrow was blocking the alley.

'Bin a pleasure a-makin' of your acquaintance, miss. Shall us be introduced, like? I be Merry-Andrew, 'tis my own barrow, and this is my good friend Mole 'ere, wondrous fast with a spade, and 'ere's old Spoon; 'e's got the sack and rope – best scooper in the business.'

'I see,' said Joanna. 'So you're builders from the new mall? I thought you were Gypsies.' She hoped this wasn't tactless, but MerryAndrew replied, proudly and cheerfully:

'Nivver, lass, neither one nor t'other. We be Resurrectionists!'

'Oh,' she said, thinking, God, one of those nutty religious sects. 'Anyway; right, well, must be get-ting along now . . .' She spoke more assertively, thrusting her trolley at them. They parted to let her through.

'Ye're a right pretty young maid,' MerryAndrew called after her, 'and plump as a partridge, to boot.

Will ye no tell us your name?'

'Joanna,' she answered, huffily. She wouldn't have described herself as plump. Hurrying round the corner to Baps, she glanced back, and had the momentary illusion that Mole was poised over Gammon Steaks with a raised shovel.

None of Joanna's friends was invited to the barbecue. 'This is a civilised do,' her dad had said. 'Sophisticated. But I suppose you're old enough to be a help, handing round nibbles and so on. If you're good.'

'Unpaid waitress, you mean,' Joanna grumbled. At eight o'clock, when the doorbell started ringing, her parents were launching the usual barbecue argument . . .

MUM: They'll all get food poisoning. Why didn't you light it earlier?

DAD: You know quite well. I had to pop out for some Pimm's.

MUM: Yes, you always do that, don't you? Wait till five minutes before a party to do a tour of the off-licences.

DAD: Well, at least I'm not still in the bath, five minutes before a party!

. . . so Joanna found herself answering the door, pouring drinks, slicing rolls. When there was a lull she took a bowl of Phileas Foggs through the patio windows onto the lawn. Up the hill, the sunset was ebbing to warm green splashed with pink; a few soap flakes of cirrus gathered behind the supermarket. She could hear the rooks calling in the clear air. The last rays of sun Day-Glo'd the grass till its points bristled emerald against the barbecue Dad had built.

77

And what a barbecue! Next best thing to an Aztec temple, it was pyramid-shaped, with three steps leading to the sacrificial grilling rack. Joanna watched her father mount to the top step; he was wearing the ceremonial apron, which depicted a torso in lacy underwear. Turning hamburgers with a fish slice in his left hand, he waved a glass of wine in the other, emphasising some point he was making to Geoff Brundell.

Joanna threaded through the guests. They were having the usual barbecue chat, sussing out each other's status. Showing off, that's what adult parties are for, she decided. How much more fun they'd have with a conjurer and a bouncy castle.

'We went to Thailand last summer,' Mr Pritchard was telling the Ryecarts, over her head.

'Crunchies?' she offered.

'Thank you, Joanna. Yes,' he resumed, 'wonderful scenery, quite unspoiled. Too far for your average tourist, y'see. And y'selves?'

'Hang-gliding,' Jane Ryecart trumped him. 'Don't suppose you've ever tried it?'

'*We* went to Portugal,' said Joanna, but no one was listening, so she went to the end of the garden and sat on the swing to finish the crisps.

The rooks spilled across the sky, flung like tea leaves on the sunset over the supermarket's clock tower; as Joanna swung dreamily back and forth, watching them, the sun sank.

'Pssst! Little miss.'

It came from the gate to the back lane. Reluctantly she looked round. Sure enough, lurking behind the hedge were the foul shapes of MerryAndrew, Mole and Spoon. With them was the barrow with the rope and sack, like silly props for a parents' race on Sports Day.

MerryAndrew was beckoning to her, his knotted hands, for all it was July, in fingerless woollen gloves. Joanna walked up to the gate, blinking away the scarlet after-image of the sun.

'I'm sorry,' she said. 'We're not at all religious here. I'm not even christened.' The last thing one needs for a fun party, she thought, is gate-crashing Jehovah's Witnesses.

The men ignored her. They were bobbing excitedly, peering past her at the barbecue. MerryAndrew hooked his finger at her again, and whispered behind his hand:

'Are they clean?'

'What?' said Joanna.

'Have they the pox? Or the pestilence?'

'Well,' said Joanna weakly, 'if you're worried about BSE, we've sausages ... and chicken legs, and frankfurters; a few chops – '

'Chops! Aye, chops!' the three exclaimed to each other. 'With the teeth still in 'em?' they demanded.

'I'm sorry,' Joanna said, more resolutely, 'but I don't have a clue what you're talking about. I think you'd better leave.'

'Molars be worth a pretty penny. Ye can at least spare us a jawbone or two, sweet wee lass.' Spoon tilted his head in an endearing manner, attempted an appealing smile, and leaned towards her over the gate. He smelled as if he'd gone off, and a cloud of flies fussed round his hat. She found herself gazing into his eyes, and saw her own tiny reflection, swimming black against the flames writhing on the cloudy curved mirror of his eye. Flames? She turned in dread, and saw as the Resurrectionists saw . . .

No garden. No house, even, no estate, but bleak heathland rolling up a hill. At the summit an outcrop of rock, a mob of trees against the moon. Also a gallows, from which a clutch of bodies hung. Some were caged in iron hoops, which served as perches for the rooks, sleepily shuffling their wings. And before her, a bonfire towered. Dark figures toiled rhythmically, building up the fire, piling it high, higher, with corpses. As the heat contracted muscles, the cadavers squirmed; there was an occasional popping sound as flesh split. A woman tumbled from the top of the pile, her limbs bouncing as she rolled to Joanna's feet. Locks of fire circled her face, like a medieval drawing of the sun; they illuminated her glaring eyes, her swollen, lolling tongue.

'Just that one body, sweet Jo. Our pretty Anna?'

The girl felt a scream knot her throat but no sound came. She gasped for air, wheezing, and felt her pockets for the inhaler, but she'd left it in the house. Wherever that was.

'What ails thee?' she heard, as blackness tightened; she fell to her knees.

On her back, she fought for breath.

'It's an asthma attack!' she heard. 'Quick. Is anyone under the limit?'

Through the nausea she was aware of a siren, of being lifted onto a stretcher, into the ambulance, of a plastic mask being jammed on her face. She opened her eyes and saw the smoked windows swaying. There was a Bart Simpson poster stuck on the ambulance ceiling, the yellow face grinned down at her; then she remembered the bonfire, and struggled to push the mask off.

'Hold her down!' a voice said. 'She's panicking.

A muscle relaxant, perhaps . . .'

Her arm stung, and darkness closed again.

When Joanna came to, she thought, at first, that she was dead. White cloaked her, cool and smooth; then she heard Mole speak.

''Tis well worth three guineas.'

A cultured voice replied, 'For a mere child? As you know very well, the rate is six shillings for the first foot, and then nine pennies per inch thereafter. That makes . . . two guineas in all, by my reckoning.'

Spoon, it sounded like, pleaded ingratiatingly, 'But doctor, she be so fresh, just take a look; never been under earth at all, sir, why, them cheeks is rosy as pippins.'

'Off with you, rogues, before I ask how you came by her. Two pound and ten shillings is my last offer. Take it; go.'

The voice swelled commandingly, ringing with authority. It was, Joanna thought, the voice of the sort of person who would put things right. A doctor. He'd soon make sense of everything.

'Come, gentlemen,' he was saying, in that reassuring bedside manner, 'let us proceed. Today I shall evulse the great vessels of the thoracic cavity from the transverse septum, incising the phrenic nerves, and lead through the tricuspid orifice to the chordae tendineae.'

A shadow flowed up the whiteness, and a pair of hands folded back the sheet. A draft chilled Joanna's naked body. Her fixed eyes saw tier upon tier of young men in black coats; they leaned forwards attentively.

'Indeed, my friends,' the surgeon went on

enthusiastically, 'the rascals spoke truly. 'Tis a peach of a specimen.'

Joanna strained to move, to cry out, but her muscles would not obey. A face framed in whiskers leaned intently above her, light flickering about its wiry outline, twinkling in its curls. Round, bright spectacles sealed the eyes. The lips pursed in concentration, and she saw a scalpel flash briefly, before, with delicate precision, it bisected her chest.

Author's note: In the old days, medical students learned their craft on corpses supplied by grave robbers, who were known as 'sack-em-up men' or 'resurrectionists'.

BERSERKER

Ashleigh was going through his routine for getting out of school. 'It's only a sore throat, Mum,' he was saying, 'and perhaps a bit of a temperature. But don't you worry about me. Your work's more important.' He was looking appealing, bringing on my urge to kick his bottom.

'He's not ill,' I chipped in. 'I saw him sliding down the banisters. And he took some biscuits – check his pockets.'

I gave him my nasty grin, and left for school. Wanted to be there early, so's I could collect the dinner money off the other little ones as they went in. It's protection money, I tell them: if I get it, they're protected from having to eat school dinners. I like to sit on the wall by the school gates waiting for them.

Jamie Berens was the first, wobbling along on his bike.

'Where's the cash, then?' I called down.

'I forgot it, Marc. Sorry.'

I jumped down and bent his thumb back till it nearly touched his wrist. Then I said, 'Bet it's in your shoes. Go on, shake 'em out.' Two pound

84

coins rolled circles on the pavement.

'Pick 'em up. Right. And give 'em here. I don't want to see that sort of behaviour again. It's disgusting, putting money next to your sweaty socks. Not to mention the deceit of it.'

I get a lot of my ideas on control from teachers. A particularly handy phrase is 'see me after school'. Gives them the whole day to get in a panic, so I've got the psychological advantage. Psychological control is very important, and just as much fun as physical. When it was Jack's party, for instance, and he was going to take the whole class swimming, I just went round saying, 'Oh, any party of Jack's is bound to be crud. I'm not going; are you?' So only his best friend turned up. They'd booked a pool, and ordered pizzas, too! Nyah, nyah, nyah. Which reminds me . . . must get that friend in my gang. Isolating the target is a prime method.

When I'd collected the dinner money (I was wearing my two-tone baggies with the long pockets), I went into class for register. Thursdays are cool. It's art first, which gives me plenty of scope to make the teacher miserable and disrupt the lesson while pretending to do my best.

'Who, me?' I always say, innocently spreading my hands. I've actually complained to the Head that the art teacher victimises me.

At first break I saw my wimp of a brother crossing the yard to the sheds. Ashleigh – what a name, I ask you! But that's typical of mothers, haven't a clue what goes on. Ash was wearing this pink and purple ski jacket Mum had bought him, and if there's one thing calculated to infuriate me, it's a Bri-nylon ski jacket from C&A.

'Where d'you think you're off to?' I demanded,

grabbing the hood.

'Indeed,' Ashleigh said, as if considering the question. 'Where am I going? Where are you going? Why, in fact, are we here at all?'

He was in one of his silly moods, so I shook him a bit. 'What are you on about?'

'Exactly,' Ashleigh continued. 'That's my point. What is any of us about? Do we, in fact, exist?'

'You'll know you exist all right when I thump you,' I said, thrusting my nose close to his.

'No,' said Ash philosophically, 'I'll know *you* exist.' He swung his rucksack round, smashing it into my shins. 'Now you know I exist!' He started to run.

I got him to the ground and banged his head against the concrete – I'll knock the cockiness out of him, if it's the last thing I do. Then I pulled him up and gave him a kick so he went stumbling across the yard.

'Don't get facey with me. You go tell your mate Rex I want to play his console. And I want it, like, now, you lippy little bastard.'

So I sat on the bike shed playing Super Mario till the bell rang. The sudden shrill of it made me drop the console off the roof. Rex picked it up and jabbed at the buttons.

'You've bust it!' he cried indignantly. 'And it was brand new.'

'You're full of shit,' I said. 'Needs a new battery, is all.' He was snivelling.

I climbed down and went to join the rest of my form. We had Social Responsibility Hour next, when we visit the old folk in Claremont. Bring a little youth and joy into their drab lives, nyah, nyah, nyah. Learn about caring. I ask you!

86

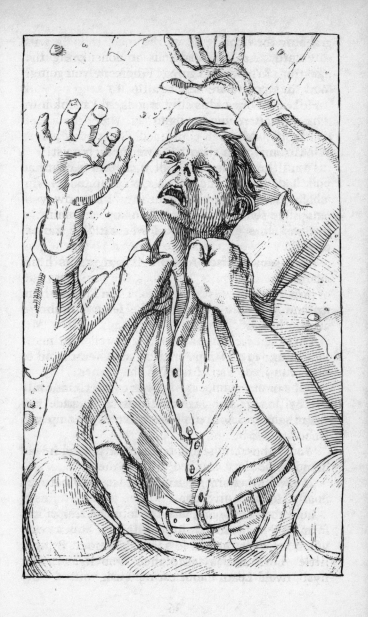

I love swaggering down the road, though, with my entourage. I'm head and shoulders taller than the rest of the class, due to being kept back a year, and they practically have to run to keep up with me. I feel like a shark with a shoal of minnows wriggling after me, trying to get where the action is; the bloodshed.

Matron, I won't say welcomed us, but showed us into the sun lounge, where the old people had just had coffee. There was a row of chairs, all wipable orange padded plastic, in a row along the wall; and there the old folks were lined up, slumped like victims of a firing squad. I was heading for Mr Maloney – we'd had a safe game of poker the previous week – but Matron tapped me on the shoulder.

'We've a new resident,' she said, 'who I'm sure would love to meet you.' Her voice rose to a shout. 'A charming young lady called Mrs Vickers.'

'Young lady?' I muttered, as she steered me to the crumpled heap of flesh in the corner.

'One of our younger girls, aren't you, Gran? Only eighty, and we've an age range past a hundred.' Her voice sank to a normal pitch. 'Haven't got our teeth in today, I fear.'

As I lowered myself into the chair beside the old woman, her face cranked towards me.

It was like a horror video; no, it was worse – even John Carpenter might shrink from this. Curtains of skin draped her collar, as if the face had slipped off. The only recognisable human feature was a nose; it was as if lips and eyes had been sucked into the skull. The mouth was a ploughed crack, and as for the eyes, well – a million radiating crazed lines centred in craters where there were just two white, puckered scars. She had no eyes.

'You'll have to speak up,' Matron was saying, 'her hearing's not quite the ticket.' I started to rise, but Matron's hand on my shoulder kept me in the chair. I looked back at the woman. 'Er . . . Hi!' I said.

The crevice under the nose quivered and split, like a wound reopening, and curled across the skin – I could see wet purple knobbles squirming inside it. A purse of worms.

'Why, she's smiling, aren't you, Gran?' Matron yelled. 'I bet a wee kiss on the cheek from a nice young man wouldn't go amiss, eh?'

I sprang up, knocking the chair back so it clattered into the patio window. I was off. Through the sun lounge, the TV lounge, the hall, out through the front door and into the fresh air.

I felt contaminated. Thank Christ old age isn't catching. I put my hands into my pockets to stop them shaking, and strolled off down the road. It felt strange being on my own, without the gang. Uncomfortably quiet. And, to tell the truth, I was shaken by my loss of nerve. Thinking about it, I decided I'd freaked out because, under this macho exterior, I'm quite a sensitive person.

First stop on the way back to school is the Asian mini-mart, because there's only one girl works there, and she's pregnant. Usually I send Joe and Leanne in, but of course they were still at the home. As I filled my pockets with Cadbury's Creme Eggs, I was wondering how I'd explain to everyone why I'd run off in a funk like that. Then I caught the assistant watching me in the curved mirror.

'Excuse me – ' she began.

I was out the door. Glancing over my shoulder, I saw her thin brown face at the window, framed by special-offer posters. I took what was left of a Creme Egg out of my mouth and hurled it. There was a 'splat', with, like, pukey dribbles down the glass. Nyah, nyah. A mouthful of chocolate spluttered down my chin with laughing, and I leapfrogged along a row of bollards till I got to McDonald's. Felt better, now.

When I came out with a pack of fries I saw the backs of a pair of familiar heads poking up over a bench. Rex and Ashleigh. I smiled to myself, seeing the back of Rex's head. It's easy to get the fat kids, and kids with glasses or silly names, but Rex – handsome, generous, kind – had been trickier. Then I'd come up with 'Say, have you ever noticed the shape of the back of Rex's head? He must be some kind of retard.' Not that there's anything wrong with his head; I should be in advertising.

Sucking softly at a fry I prowled, creeping up behind them. I was gonna grab their collars, get them in real trouble for bunking school. Then I heard Rex say . . .

'We've got to do something.'

'Impossible,' Ashleigh said. 'He's got the place running like a dictator state. Informers everywhere.'

'And torturers,' Rex agreed. 'It's that dreadful laugh of his that gets me. Like a cartoon baddy. Perhaps he thinks he's Ming the Merciless.'

'What I can't bear is the way bullies like him get off scot-free. I mean, Marc does whatever he wants and doesn't give a stuff what anyone thinks, so you can't hurt him. That's his strength. It's not 'cause he's big, it's 'cause he doesn't care about people. And I've got to live with him!'

'Never mind,' Rex consoled. 'Some way or other you'll get your own back . . .' His voice drawled, 'Maybe not today, maybe not tomorrow, but some day . . .' There was a thoughtful pause. 'Hey, can't you just see him in ten years' time? Walking a pit bull, with a fag over one ear and a dart over the other.'

They giggled. 'Nah,' Ashleigh groaned. 'Worse still. He's planning to join the army, Gawd help us. The berserker with the bazooka.'

They were laughing too hard to hear my footsteps. I leaned between them.

'Guess who!' I said quietly and smiled, my eyes sliding from one frozen face to the other. Our cheeks were almost touching. 'May I share the joke?' I asked, and walked slowly round the bench to stand before them, my thumbs in my belt. There was that glorious surge of power coursing down my nerves, tingling my fingertips, which comes the second before I lose control.

'Stand up, Ashleigh.'

I saw my hand meet the side of his head with a sound as satisfying as the thwack of tennis ball on racket. My brain was spinning, all excitement, tight, fizzing energy. Well, I told myself, it's for his own good, knocking a bit of discipline into him.

Ashleigh had gone white, his cheek red-mooned where my palm had struck. His eyes were wet and bright. Pathetic, he looked, cowering there. Little ratty, rabbity thing, deserving all it got.

'Traitor!' I hissed. 'Loyalty, that's what families are about. Looking after each other, sticking up for each other.'

Regaining my cool, I slammed my knuckles down on the top of his head – doesn't leave a mark – and punched him in the stomach. He creased to the pavement, but through the tears and snot he looked up and croaked, 'You're a real bastard, Marc.'

I put a threatening fist to his face, then gave my nasty grin, all crinkly eyes and clenched teeth.

'Nyah, nyah, nyah,' I jeered, and walked off.

Bastard and proud of it, that's me. Marc rules OK.

'Mr Crawshaw, Mr Crawshaw? Can you hear me, dear? Turn up your hearing aid. *I said, turn up your aid*. That's better. You're looking *marvellous* today. Handsome as a film star. And how are we feeling? Oh, dear. Nurse, nurse, I'm afraid Mr Crawshaw's had a little accident . . . thank you.

'All comfy now? Right, where were we? Well, first, let me introduce myself. I'm Mrs Watermark, your new caseworker. We've been thinking about you down at the office, so don't think you're being neglected! Oh, dearie me, no! We want to get you out of hospital quick smart. TLC at home's what the doctor ordered. Tender loving care. So we've been beavering away like detectives, no stone unturned, to find you a carer, and we've come up with a *wonderful* surprise!'

The other blurred shape loomed closer, light gleamed on a bald pate.

'Hello, Marc,' said Ashleigh. 'Guess who.'

MAKING AN ENTRANCE

Kate and Christine were looking for a book their mum wanted for her birthday. They'd been to the Uni bookshop and Smith's, and Menzies' and Waterstone's, but couldn't find it anywhere. By the time they'd enquired, 'Excuse me, do you have *The Female Fight Against Oppression*?' for the umpteenth time, they were getting bored, and started dreaming up titles it might be more fun to ask for. *Any Books at All*, for instance. 'What! Call yourself a bookshop, when you haven't got *Any Books at All*?'

'When I grow up,' Chris said, 'I shall write a novel about a dynasty, a blockbusting tragic tale rich in political turmoil and passion. It will be called *A Gruesome Body with Purple Pimples*. Little old ladies across the nation will rush to their local bookshop and challenge the assistant, "Tell me, young man, do you have *A Gruesome Body with Purple Pimples*?" '

'He won't care,' said Kate. 'After all, it can't be that easy to insult someone who's always being asked if he's got a Pooh collection, or a pop-up Paddington.'

They were about to go home when Kate noticed a banner between the pillars of the town hall. 'PBFA Book Fair,' it read. 'Today only.' They went up the steps and followed the crowd to a room with rows of stalls, like a marketplace, with more books than they'd ever seen.

'They're all old,' Chris grumbled, 'and they're not even in alphabetical order. How are you supposed to find anything?'

She took one down and flicked through it. The cover was dingy, but the illustrations, stuck in under tissue paper, were stunning.

'I'll have this one,' she said. 'How much?'

The man looked inside the cover. '£350.'

'Oh.'

'Try the cardboard box,' he suggested. 'See if anything takes your fancy. 50p each.'

She put her head under the table and groped in the tumble of books. They had covers missing, and enough fingerprints and suspicious stains to make a policeman very happy. There was H. K. Klingerstorff's *Judo! In Pictures*, for instance, Schulz-Kamphenkel's *The Romance of the Fungus World*, and *Modern Pig-Sticking* by A. E. Wardrop. But at the bottom, under *My Year with the Woodpeckers*, she came across a . . . well, volume is the only word for it. The cover was engraved leather, the pages thick and creamy. It was called *The Black Pullet*.

'Are you sure it's only 50p?' she asked.

'All right. A pound to you, pet. Or, if you really want to haggle, £1.50.'

'No, no. 50p is fine. Thanks very much.'

He put it in a brown paper bag, and they left. 'What would Mum want with a book about hens?' said Kate, as they queued for the bus.

'Doesn't matter what it's about. It's the most beautiful book I've ever seen. Why, it must be hundreds of years old.'

They climbed the bus stairs and swayed to the front. Chris couldn't resist taking it out of the bag. She blew off the dust and turned the title page.

'The Hen with the Golden Eggs,' she read out, 'comprising the Science of Magical Talismans and Rings, the Art of Necromancy, for the Conjuration of Aerial and Infernal Spirits, of Sylphs, Undines and Gnomes, serviceable for the acquisition of the Secret Sciences, and for the Discovery of Treasures.'

'What a mouthful!' said Kate. 'Is it science?'

'Don't you realise? It's magic.' Chris stroked the cover, then raised the book to her face and sniffed it. 'Power, that's what it's about. Power and money.' She turned the pages.

'You mean black magic? Calling up the Devil?'

'That's right. We'll give Mum flowers instead.'

Kate leaned across to read. 'It's evil,' she said, and yanked it from her sister's hands. A second later she was jamming it through the window. Chris wrenched her arm back, but it was too late – the book bounced onto the road and lay there, its pages rippling. Chris swore, ran along the bus and clattered down the stairs. The bus was moving as she jumped, and she fell on her hands. Rows of faces turned to watch her crawl in the gutter, scrabbling through the cans and orange peel to rescue the book, as the bus swung round the corner.

'Shh! Get some clothes on. We're going to the playground.'

'I'm asleep,' Kate murmured.

95

'The sooner you do what I want, the sooner you'll be back in bed. Tell you what – it's a midnight feast.' Chris threw a tracksuit at her.

'You're a lunatic!' She yawned, looking at her watch. 'I don't know why I put up with you.'

'Because you're a wimp,' Chris said, 'and nothing ever happens in your life unless I make it.'

They let themselves out of the front door and ran the three streets to the woods. There, leaves flailed overhead as trees stirred the darkness. Chris got the torch from her rucksack and they followed the dot of light along the path.

In its lonely clearing, the playground looked enchanted; the moon was knocking sparks off the swing chains, silver-dipping the climbing frame, the seesaws and roundabouts as if it was Christmas. Kate whooped and ran up the slide.

'Don't be childish. We've business to attend to,' called Chris.

'Have you brought nice things to eat?' Kate slithered back.

'No. There's nothing to eat.' Chris got the book out of the rucksack. 'Try to think about something other than your stomach.'

The pages glowed beneath her fingers – she didn't even need the torch. 'We're here to try and find our heart's desire. Come and see. You shouldn't be frightened, it's really just a recipe book. Here's a fun spell: "How to cause the Appearance of Three Ladies or Three Gentlemen in One's Room after Supper".'

Kate looked over her sister's shoulder. 'How bizarre,' she said. 'Why would anyone want to do that?'

They hunched over the book, their shoulders

96

pressed together.

'As far as I can make out,' she said at last, 'it's all silly. For instance, to become invisible you have to get up before sunrise on a Wednesday and get seven black beans, three candles and a spoon. Fair enough. But then it's "take the head of a dead man and sprinkle with excellent brandy".'

'You mean, where would we get the brandy?'

'I mean, all the recipes start off sensibly, then there's an impossible ingredient. That's because they know it'll never work.'

'You're probably right. Look at this one: "Find a boy of nine years, cleanly dressed and of good behaviour." I still think it's worth a try, though; and this is the perfect place for a pentacle.'

Chris took a plastic spade from the sandpit and cut two interesting triangles in the sand.

'Please don't,' Kate said. 'What would Mum say?'

'Shut up and make yourself useful. Get rid of those ice-cream papers.'

The wind was rising, and the swings chinked and swayed at their moorings, the roundabout clanking against its metal mast.

'You just want an audience,' Kate muttered. 'How's the Devil supposed to see that thing anyway, with your footprints all over the place?' She watched her sister walk to the centre of the pentacle, hold up the book, and turn towards the moon.

'O spirit,' Chris called out, 'I adjure thee by Ariel, Aqua and Arios, and their power by which the elements are overthrown, the earth moves . . .' Her voice rang out, '. . . and all the hosts of things celestial, of things terrestrial, of things infernal do tremble and are confounded together; speak to me

97

visibly.' She held out her arms. 'Come, why dost thou tarry? Christine Kunz commands thee.'

Dimly she heard Kate: 'It's pathetic. A girl in a Take That tracksuit talking to herself in a playground!' Chris opened her eyes and saw the scared face, stoatlike in the sharp, white light.

'I'm going now, whether you come or not,' Kate shouted.

She envies the power of my imagination, Chris thought, always has done. As the gate slammed, she shut Kate out of her mind.

'I invoke, conjure and command thee, O spirit, to appear and show thyself before this circle, in fair and comely shape, without deformity or guile.' The book trembled in her hands, but she went on, fiercely. 'I command thee, by the sea of glass, by the four beasts having eyes before and behind, do thou perform my desires!'

The leaves above hissed, disintegrating and reforming on a patch of sky, which clenched itself into whirling cloud. She felt a thread of saliva dribble from her open mouth, and wiped it away. The playground was fused with the sky, merging in ecstatic motion; they were alive and she was part of them.

And then, at last, the wind wailed, 'Lo, I am here! What dost thou seek of me? Why dost thou disturb my repose? Answer me.'

Against the pallid cloud the slide was mere outline, but she saw a form solidify in the cage at the top and pulse loosely through the bars. She shaded her eyes.

'It is my wish to make a pact with thee, so as to obtain wealth and genius at thy hands.'

A gust whipped across the tarmac, shaking out

sand, bowling a paper cup.

'One gift alone,' it shrieked, 'and that in barter that thou shall give thyself to me in fifty years to do with, body and soul, as I please.'

Chris's heart flipped painfully, a double beat of terror.

She took an exercise book and biro out of her rucksack; angling the book to the light, she wrote a contract and tore out the page. Something slopped down the slide.

A youth jumped to his feet. His leather jacket was studded and chained as if part of the playground equipment, a starry addition to the glitter. He drew a knife from his pocket and plucked out the blade with his teeth. She watched him toss it in the air; it spun three bright circles before landing on the roundabout, quivering in the wood.

Chris walked over and tugged it free. Crouched in his shadow between the steel rails, she held the blade above her hand. After a moment, she drew the edge over her skin and watched the beads of blood well in a row, then trickle blackly to the white valley of her palm. She dipped the point of the knife and scrawled this devil's ink across the paper. The boy held the rails, penning her in the wooden triangle. His face was shadowed; she could only see his cheek hump in a grin as he began to run with the roundabout, faster and faster, spinning her till her hair shredded round her face, in her mouth, so that trees, a bench, gate, hut, flicked past again, again, and the paper twirled away in the wind . . .

The roundabout churned to stillness, and she was alone.

Chris sat in a bookstore. The table before her bore a pile of glossy hardbacks, the height of which happily matched the length of the queue. It was a tall pile, Chris's novels being as thick as Dickens's. Or as two short planks, Kate might have said, though she was now agent and manager to her sister.

'Smile!' she whispered in Chris's ear. 'Do at least try to be civil.' Kate has never appreciated that it's talent that makes work sell, not charm, Chris thought. Dashing off another signature, she admired its streamlined chassis, its aerodynamic point; Kate's signature was, she considered, more rusty and upright, with a basket at the front.

'Thanks so much,' Chris addressed her public. 'Do hope you enjoy it.' Yet another hand slid her book across the table. She flipped back the flyleaf and saw a sheet of lined paper.

'I, Christine Patricia Kunz, agree to sell to the bearer my soul in exchange for my heart's desire.'

The rounded letters had a simplicity, an innocence she would never have believed possible. The sepia signature was so faded as to be almost invisible. She blinked, and the paper was gone.

'Hello, Dame Chris!' said a young man, smiling at her. 'I believe we've met before.'

'No doubt.' She gripped her pen. 'In my travels I come across a great many people.' She smiled insincerely. 'And as you see, there are a great many people waiting their turn behind you, so we'd better say goodbye.' There was something wrong with his eyes.

'*Au revoir*, then.' He winked, and disappeared into the crowd.

Chris felt shaky and slightly sick. 'Kate,' she

whispered, 'I've had enough for today. Call the limo.'

'But you've another hour's signing!'

'They'll buy the book anyway. And I don't believe in letting people take advantage of my good nature.'

Seeing the black band of car slide across the bookshop window, Chris rose. A path cleared through her admirers. 'So sorry,' she said, 'but I'm due at a première.' Kate held the door while her sister walked elegantly through. 'Making an exit with style,' she had often told Kate, 'is as important as making an entrance. Grooming and poise are what matter.'

The chauffeur held the limo door, and Chris sank onto the rear seat, drawing her legs in. She could see Kate, red-faced and hair unravelled, through the shop window. The manager was gesticulating at her.

'The Plaza,' Chris directed the chauffeur, as she relaxed. 'I've got a première tonight, and the Plaza is not only the best hotel in London but it is situated over the cinema, so I shall be able to appear looking my best. You're new, aren't you?' The back of his head seemed unfamiliar. When you're as well known as I am, she thought, you can't always remember staff because, well, one tends to avoid eye contact – all contact, really – with the great unwashed.

He changed gear and turned his head so that the peaked cap slotted into view in the mirror; his eyes were gold.

'Come on, old girl, you must know me. I've been driving you for years.'

Even though the car was moving, Chris tugged

the door handle. It was locked. Outside the hermetically sealed bubble, the public swilled greyly, silently by.

'We'll be there in a tick,' said the chauffeur. The car drew up, and he leapt to open the passenger door.

'I shall be complaining to the car-hire company,' she said. 'You are an insolent young man.'

Chris swept up the hotel steps without tipping him. She refused to be intimidated by a figment of her imagination.

'Evening, madam,' said the desk clerk, but Chris couldn't be bothered to reply, and headed for the lift. She pressed the button and waited for the ornamental iron box to crank down. It was playing 'Moon River'. The operator folded the grille gates back, and she stepped in.

'Which floor, madam?'

'Twentieth,' she told him. 'The penthouse suite.' She looked at the carpet – burgundy, with a diamond pattern – and became aware of the boy's green uniform: crisp trouserlegs with a ribbon stripe down the side, from under which peeped a pair of tufted hooves. Slowly she looked up. His eyes were gold, with black slits for pupils.

She lurched across and pressed the button.

'Your time hasn't come yet, madam,' he said, but she dragged back the doors as the lift juddered and was still. She ran down the corridor, her feet floating on the carpet. At the stairs she looked back down the perspective of doors, and saw his head angled from the bright lift, watching her.

Chris took off her shoes and ran up the stairs. The sharp red heels clacked together in time with her panting.

Sixteenth floor. Fire door. Seventeenth floor. Fire door. On each landing an identical corridor – an infinity of locked doors and one repro side table with flower arrangement and mirror. As she burst onto the top floor, she crammed the shoes under her arm to fumble for the key. She unlocked and slammed the door. The air was suffocating and she felt the make-up drip down her face. The curtains were drawn, the sheet turned back, with two round chocolate mints on the pillow.

Chris reached through the curtains to open the window, but her false nails became enmeshed with a net curtain which was secured over the window, sealing her in. She ripped it down, but couldn't open the window, so she dialled room service.

'Don't you have air conditioning in this hellhole? Let me tell you, this is the last time I'll be staying here. Send up a stiff gin. No, make that a bottle. And maybe some smoked salmon.'

She pasted her cheeks with face-pack and put rollers in her hair in order to look her best for the evening. There might be just enough time to phone her therapist . . . not, as she told herself, that I'm mentally at all unstable, it's just that with all the pressure I'm under, well, I do need someone to talk to.

'Room service.'

She opened the door, and the boy pushed in a trolley. There was a silver bowl of fruit salad and a bottle of champagne in an ice bucket.

'Compliments of the management, with apologies for any inconvenience,' he said, and wedged the champagne between his knees, pushing the cork with his thumbs. As he stooped, his cap tumbled off, and nesting in the curls Chris saw a pair of gnarled horns.

The cork sprang out. He poured a glass for her, and another for himself.

'I think this calls for a celebration,' he said. She backed towards the bed. She was feeling stressed, but knew her pills were in the bathroom. A pain in her left wrist flowered up her arm, extending tendrils into her chest.

'The impertinence!' she moaned. 'Get out.'

'Look at it this way,' he said. 'If you find a pinta on the doorstep every morning, you shouldn't be surprised when the milkman comes a-calling with the bill.'

He was holding that grubby bit of lined paper up, and she could see a list of French verbs on the back. She stood up and grabbed at it – a torn contract is null and void. As he snatched it away, he laughed.

The pain circled her heart, stabbing rhythmically, making her sick, and she found herself heaving into the ice bucket. She wiped her mouth on the napkin, smearing her lipstick, then lunged at him, at the tantalising bit of paper dangling between finger and thumb.

This time the pain squeezed her heart tightly, as if to wring out the last drop of blood. She fell to the carpet. There was a banging in her ears, and the room distorted as though it were a goldfish bowl. She was sick again, this time on the carpet, and inch by inch crawled through the mess towards the boy. He was kneeling, jiggling the contract at her.

'What a silly, superstitious woman you are!' he teased.

'Well, you're here, aren't you? Come for my soul?'

' "*Alterius non sit qui suus esse potest*" is my

motto. Make yourself what you will. And you have.
Those hatchet biographies and tacky best sellers
made you one of the wealthiest women in the
world. Never mind the careers you ruined, the
family you neglected. That charity for children
which gave you not only publicity, but a villa in
Nice . . .'

'We needed an office,' she pleaded.

'. . . the blackmail you used to make doors open,
and to gain political influence . . . I really should
congratulate you. A most diligent worker on the
Devil's behalf; in fact, your account is fully paid.
There isn't the slightest spot of virtue left on your
soul. Your receipt, madam.'

He ripped the paper to shreds and let them loose
over her head. She felt them curl around her rollers,
stick to her face-pack.

'Who are you?' she whimpered.

'With your heart condition,' he said, 'probably a
hallucination due to the constriction of blood vessels leading to the brain. Or your conscience. Does
it matter?'

'Please go away. There is a première I am due to
attend. My first screenplay. I shall be late.' She saw
the silver wheels of the trolley, and, ignoring the
pain, dragged herself up its framework. She stood
for a moment leaning on it as if it were a zimmer
frame.

Her vision blurred – perhaps it was only due to
a lost contact lens. The mauve curtains with pink
flowers seemed to wrinkle into a whirlpool round
the bedspread. The boy leapt onto the bed, swam
into the vortex. She had the illusion his limbs were
shrinking, his body bloating in a squat ooze of hairy
flesh among the pillows. A claw picked the silver

paper off the chocolate mints, which were ingested.

'Kate,' she called. 'Mother. I don't feel very well.' Her heart bulged like an octopus, flicking tentacles of agony through her veins. As she put more weight on the trolley, she felt her arms crumple. Her face slapped down on the garish orange salmon, splattering pineapple, guava, cherries.

The thing on the bed laughed, peals of derision bouncing round the soundproof cell.

'My fruity beauty,' it squealed, 'don't let me keep you; don't let me disappoint your fans.'

She tried to heave herself off the trolley, but as she raised her head she met, nose to nose, a face so inhuman she was surprised it could express such glee. It vanished, and the curtains swelled at her, reaching like arms – she felt the trolley slide, gather speed and sail towards the window.

On impact, splinters rained brightly into the night and cold splashed her arms, sucked at her cheeks. The trolley teetered half in, half out of the window.

And so she was finally there, at the edge of the abyss, staring down. Many were the fires of Hell crisscrossing their grid across the dark city. Horns cried out, and sirens, and the damned too, as they simmered along the red carpet to the cinema and scurried under the awning, that long canvas serpent aglow with television lights.

The trolley slipped and she screamed. It scraped on metal a little further. Then it tilted one last fraction and she was toppling beyond hope, plunging down, her skirt whipped inside out like an umbrella in a gale, flapping as furiously as a collapsed parachute, and she couldn't hold it down as she plummeted faster, much faster than it seems in films, down ... down ... couldn't cover her legs ... or breathe ...

She glimpsed royal faces raised in wonder just before she hit the canopy.

'Sorry,' said the bookseller. 'Why don't you have a dig through the junk?'

The girl browsed past Mudie's *Feathered Trikes of the British Islands*, Mendell's *Who's Who of Basketball* and a heap of lurid tomes by someone called Chrystelle P. Kunz, until she came upon an exquisite leather ... well, volume is the only word.

MAROONED

I'm dead lucky, I realise that. Living in this premier road. With our own tennis court and swimming pool and everything. It's just that when I'm home from Eton, Mum's away deep-sea diving in Florida, Dad's in Brussels, and it gets a bit quiet sometimes. The au pair's always out, and anyway, my Norwegian's not up to much. This is a classy area, where the neighbours keep themselves to themselves – the only time I met one was when a lady in a nightdress came hammering on our door; it turned out that her husband had been hitting her, but she was from an embassy and they've got diplomatic immunity, so I gave her a cup of coffee, and she went home.

Anyway, the day this story started, I was at a loose end, as Consuela doesn't come to clean on Tuesdays. When the doorbell rang, I thought it might be the girl come to change the flower arrangements; I ran to the study to check with the entryviewer, and there on the screen was a man with a beard and long hair, sort of biblical-looking.

'Who is it?' I said into the entryphone.

''S Gerry,' he said. 'I always comes of a Tuesday

mornin'. Madam gives me ten quid regular of a Tuesday.'

'Are you with Avant Gardeners?' I said. 'Ursula's supposed to pay you. She'll be back at seven.' I turned off the entryscreen and started playing my Game-Gear, but the bell kept ringing. I went downstairs and opened the door.

''S Gerry,' he said again. 'Me Giro's not come. Got nothin' to eat, see. Or drink.'

Now I could see him properly – oily ropes of hair, splitting, toadlike boots – and smell him, I realised that he was one of Mum's good causes. She's a very caring person, always off to charity balls.

'Would you like a sandwich?' I asked. 'Or, I think there are some vol-au-vents in the fridge.'

'Tell the truth, I'm thirsty rather than hungry. Got a drink to spare?'

'Well . . .' I said doubtfully, 'I could make us a cup of tea, I suppose. It's just that Mum's gone deep-sea di – er, gone to Waitrose.' (In fact, we order our groceries from the deli, but I didn't want him to know she was away.)

'All alone, are yer? Well, I'll pop in for a minute, if yer askin'.'

Before I knew it, he was in the hall. I led the way into the sitting room, and he lowered himself onto a sofa. It's leather, I told myself, Consuela should be able to sponge it down.

'Nice place you got 'ere,' he was saying, leaning over to rub the silk drapes between finger and thumb. 'Quality fabric, these curtains. I 'preciate a bit of quality.'

'They're festoons,' I said. 'Not curtains.' Averting my eyes from the sores on his knuckles – some redly open, others yellow-scabbed – I went out to

the kitchen. I made a pot of real coffee, put it on a tray with cake and biscuits, and carried it to the sitting room. Standing in the doorway, I felt a stab of incredulity at the sight before me – acres of pastel carpeting, marble coffee table, statue lamps, rag-rolled walls, everything interior-designed to the nth degree – and there, in the midst of three metres of pale-pink sofa, it looked as if someone had just emptied a dustbin. But I have been brought up not to make value judgements on the less fortunate.

'White, with sugar?' I asked.

'Irish,' he said. 'D'ye not know how to make it? Never mind, I already found your drinks cabinet.'

Sure enough, there was a bottle of whisky tucked between his boots. I noticed, uncomfortably, that his pockets were bulgier than when I'd left the room. He stirred his coffee, put the teaspoon in his pocket, and bit into a piece of chocolate cake. 'Where are you from?' I asked, politely.

'That's a long story, boy. Roehampton, to start with. Was in the building trade for a while, but I likes it better on the road. Got me freedom, me mates and that. I could tell yer some tales . . .'

'Go on, then,' I said.

So he poured himself another drink and talked of outwitted policemen, windfalls from the backs of lorries, a game of cards played to win a lady. 'Though it's hard, too, mind yer. Gets so cold some nights, takes yer half an hour next mornin' to check ye're still alive . . .' He coughed expansively, and wiped his beard on his sleeve. 'Time I was off, boy. Ye're a gent. Thanks for the grub.'

He lurched up from the depths of the sofa and shuffled to the door.

'Thank you for coming,' I said. 'I enjoyed it.'

'My pleasure,' he said. 'Oh, and about that little matter . . .'

'What matter?'

'The ten quid madam always gives me. If it's no trouble.' He held his palm out.

I went into the study and got cash from the desk drawer. When I got back he was on the step, shifting from foot to foot, eager to be off.

'Ta muchly,' he said, pocketing it in his inner overcoat. 'And what's your name, squire?'

'Daniel.'

'Ye're a pal, Daniel.' He shook me warmly by the hand. I watched him sidle down the drive, then I shut the door and went to the cloakroom to scrub my fingers.

Next Tuesday I was ready for him, with the tenner in an envelope. It seemed a less embarrassing way of making a donation. I'd also made a nice little lunch pack with a slice of quiche and some Brie sandwiches. I'd been thinking about asking him in again, but I didn't think Dad would be too pleased about the depletion of his silver snuffbox collection.

When the bell rang, I ran down to open the door. It was raining, and his hair had silver spiderwebs of drops all over it. Rivulets of rain made clean tracks down his face and dripped from the end of his nose. His porous features, sprouting knobbly as toadstools, steamed damply.

'I'm afraid I can't invite you in today,' I said, 'but here's your . . . present.' I put the parcel and envelope into his hands. They looked grotesquely like a birthday presentation, with silver foil gift-wrapping and accompanying card. His eye pouches clenched.

'What, got the vicar comin' to tea, 'ave we? Well, thanks anyway, Little Lord Fauntleroy!'

As he stomped down the drive he extracted the money, then tossed the envelope and lunch pack into the fountain. I closed the door and went to wash my hands. It was, I admit, a little upsetting. Perhaps I should have asked him in for coffee again. The morning stretched bleakly away before me, so I went into the fitness suite to have a bounce on the trampoline.

At lunchtime I sat at the breakfast peninsula to have the rest of the quiche, and was just packing my plate and knife and fork into the dishwasher, when the bell rang.

I saw on the entryscreen it was Gerry again.

'Hello,' I said. 'What do you want?'

''S Gerry,' he said. 'I always comes of a Tuesday. Madam gis me ten pounds every Tuesday.' His speech dragged oddly.

'I know,' I said. 'I already gave it to you. Don't you remember?'

'Liar. I thought you was different, but you're just like the rest of 'em. Kick a man when 'e's down.'

'I gave you ten pounds. It was in an envelope. And a nice lunch. Don't you remember?'

He mumbled something. From the hall I heard the door shuddering, something pounding at it. I ran and quickly slotted the chain across. I wanted to get away from the door, which was shaking as if it would burst open at any moment, but there are windows on each side, and I was terrified of him seeing me. I crawled over the parquet floor and pulled myself up behind a pillar. If I could slink from pillar to pillar, I'd be able to get to the kitchen.

I peered round and caught a glimpse of a bloodshot, rolling eye at the window to the left of the door, so I quickly withdrew my head. I took a breath, then dashed to the next pillar. There was a howl from the front steps.

'I *saw* you, yer mean little bastard. Rich creep! Think I can't see you behind there, with them red ears stickin' out like Prince Charles?'

I ran into the kitchen and climbed onto the island in the middle, where I huddled with the phone. I dialled 999.

'Police, please,' I said. 'And hurry!'

'What address?'

'Elite Realm,' I whispered. '19 King's Avenue.'

'I know where King's Avenue is –'

'Then quick, please! There's a man trying to break in.'

'Yes, I know where King's Avenue is, and frankly, dear, I don't believe you live there. We are trained professionals, you see, experienced enough to know a hoax call when we hear one. So get off the line, or you'll find yourself in big trouble.'

'But –'

'There are others trying to get through. I don't want to hear from you again.' The line died. I became aware of the dried flowers on the Smallbone ceiling raft hanging round my face, and sneezed. When I opened my eyes, I saw Gerry in the garden, watching me through the kitchen window. Our eyes met, and he tried to push the window open. It's double glazed. He vanished for a few seconds, then reappeared with a croquet mallet, which he swung again and again at the window, bouncing it off the glass until finally it shattered. Then he hauled himself up onto the sill, his hulk blocking the light from the room. I crouched on the island as he began to squeeze recklessly through the glass shards; blood dripped onto our white Italian marble floor, but he didn't seem to notice. Funny how clean that blood was, such shiny, primary red. As I jumped down and ran back into the hall, I heard him behind me. 'Oh, Danny Boy,' he was singing.

I unchained the door and ran out, down the steps, past the fountain, along the drive and out into the road. Standing there in the rain, I wondered what to do. The trouble with places like King's Avenue is that they're miles from anywhere. People get about by car. I thought of hiding on the Common, but I'm not allowed to go there, because it's where the bad men go.

I felt a tear itch the side of my nose and run saltily into my mouth. Then I pulled myself together and crossed the road. The gate of the first house had an entryphone.

'Excuse me,' I said, 'I'm Daniel. I live across the road. Please could you please help me?'

The answer came in Japanese, and the gate didn't open, so I walked to the next house. This time the bell was answered by a volley of barking. After half an hour I was getting cold and discouraged, and dawdled back along the road. 'Look here, Daniel,' I told myself, 'he's not exactly in good shape, and you're a yellow belt in karate. And there's Dad's harpoon in the study. Besides, he's probably gone by now.'

The front door was shut, so I crept round the side of the house peeping through all the windows.

At the fitness room, I nearly had a heart attack; as I crouched at the windowsill, Gerry's haemorrhoidal face suddenly cannoned up like a jack-in-the-box, sank down, then sprang towards the ceiling again. His expression was joyous. When I'd recovered my cool, I realised he was trampolining. Wearing Dad's white Armani suit, too. The nerve! I thought of the way we are trained at school to have natural authority, so that we will be able to take on the responsibilities required by our place in society when the time comes.

I got in through the garage and stepped into the kitchen, my shoes crisp on broken glass. Red tracks trailed through the house across our vast and previously undefiled expanses – I had the sort of shock Robinson Crusoe might have had, encountering footprints on his desert island. Violating my territory, they were, meandering across the white marble, the yellow parquet, the pink sitting-room carpet to the fitness suite.

'Danny,' a voice echoed through the rooms. 'Are ye sure your old man gets the best whisky? Seems to disagree with me.'

I heard retching, and, looking through the doorway, I saw he'd lifted the lid of the concert grand and was leaning over it. He straightened and grinned at me.

'There's nothin' makes you feel on top of the world so much as a good 'eave. Really sets you up, so's you can party again.'

'Don't you think it's time you were going now?' I said. 'The party's over.'

He stumbled up to me and put a hand on my shoulder. 'I've got a nephew just like you,' he said. There were tears in his eyes. 'Lives in Eastbourne. He wouldn' chuck his old uncle out.'

'Why don't you go and see him, then?'

I demanded.

'I might just do that, I might, very well, just do that. Nights on the open road, under the stars. Layby caffs, egg 'n' chips. The sea front, and the waves trundling in. Winkles. You coming?'

He laid an arm round my shoulders. It was warm and heavy, smelling pleasantly of Paco Rabanne. We stood there, dreaming.

'You're crazy!' I said, pulling away. 'And you're drunk. Get out of my house!'

'All righ' then, little Mr High an' Mighty! Thinks he's so wunnerful, wee Lordy Bountiful. Master Berk-in-a-Merc, I'm off now. But, as it says on the bottle, "Afore ye go" . . .'

He grabbed the sun-terrace drinks trolley and careered across the fitness suite to the swimming pool.

'Stop that at once!' I shouted, running after him. He drew up sharply, flinging his arms in the air, and the trolley shot over the mosaic edge into the pool. The ornamental ironwork seemed to buckle and stretch through the blue water, and cocktail glasses drifted down in jellyfish spirals. Several bottles floated, bobbing in the expanding wave circle – Martini seeped redly into the blue, increasing my sense that an unstoppable accident was occurring.

'Please stop now,' I begged. 'I'm sorry if I upset you.'

'I want to stop, I really do – but I just can't resist . . . one . . . last . . .'

He began to push the grand piano towards the pool. Dad'll go spare, I thought. I mean, none of us can play it, but it looks great. And it cost a fortune. I stood the other side and pushed back. He stag-

118

gered, being unsteady on his feet, then stuck out his jaw and, scowling with concentration, pushed back even harder, edging me across the tiles. I turned my back and tried to lean against it, digging my heels in, but they skidded towards the edge.

I was falling – blue all around me, in me, liquid sky, and a great weight bearing down from above. I swam frantically, scissoring my legs to escape the piano. I could see its silky shadow gliding along the bottom of the pool. I moved in a nightmare, unable to breathe, turning in slow motion. The edge of the piano descended, pressed gently against my ankle, squeezed it to the tiles with the inexorable strength of a shark closing its jaws. Above me, light twined in and out while green bottles clinked and collided. My arms made breaststroke patterns, but it was no use. I had to breathe. Beyond the chain of bubbles slipping from my nostrils, I saw a face ripple. I closed my eyes and stretched from the depths.

Everything purpled behind my eyelids, and there was singing in my ears. Over this a muffled splash sounded, and I felt someone beside me, tugging at my foot. It popped out like a cork, and I shot to the surface. The lid of the piano came to hand, and, gasping, I clung to the wreckage. After a minute, I hauled myself onto its curved hull. I rubbed the chlorine from my eyes.

A shape in a white Armani suit floated by, drifting lazy as a cruising seagull, face down, arms outstretched. I sat for a while, resting, watching it, hands dangling between my knees.

At last, I lowered myself into the water and struck out for the shore.

RIVALS

There was much dispute about the school history trip last year. We wanted 'The Destruction of Pompeii', but the insurance was too high, and as the best historical events were for over-eighteens, we ended up with Celebrity Tours. The celebrities in the brochure looked a pretty dull bunch, all whiskers and collars. There was some enthusiasm for the Mystery Tour, but Kev said no, he'd been on one where they'd got landed with some weirdo called George Eliot; face like a truck, and he'd been wearing a frilly skirt.

'Will you shut up, you little eejits!' roared Mr O'Connor. He lowered his voice and went on, 'We will make the acquaintance of Leonardo da Vinci. A grand fellow, not just a painter, but an inventor too. War machines, a sewage system – he even invented the garlic crusher. There should be something to interest everyone.'

So the next Tuesday morning we got on the coach and set off for Kilkenny to see Leonardo. The Timeport was a warehouse near Ballyragget. We paid, then bought ice creams and walked round the timeship while we ate them. It looked like a flying saucer, but a Victorian one, with rivets bolting the iron sections together, and a network of supporting struts. Functional, it was, like a small gasworks; rather disappointing when you're expecting something high-tech.

The hostess gave us a talk on good manners – 'Don't forget you will be privileged guests in a person's private home' – then we filed up the steps and through the security scan at the door. They have to be very careful; I think we all remember where we were the night Lincoln was shot.

Most kids had cameras, some had autograph books, and Kevin and I had our sketchbooks for Leonardo to sign. We consider ourselves artists and there's a lot of competition between us, though I have to admit, Kevin's work has the edge. Before that day, which changed everything, we had been planning to work on *Spitting Image*, or perhaps do the special effects in horror films.

The interior of the ship was like a theatre in the round. At the entrance there were the toilets and buffet, and rings of seats, about twenty deep, leading down to a central arena where there was a large television. We were shown a biographical video, then the TV was wheeled away and they told us to fasten our safety belts. There was a buzzing; the timeship began to tremble, and I closed my eyes as the stage pulsed sickeningly in and out of sight.

When the vibration died away I opened my eyes again and saw a ghostly sphere in the centre of the stage. It hovered, and wisps of steam snaked around it. Inside, a table appeared, with legs which rippled against a red-tiled floor. A chair materialised behind the table, then a white twirl firmed up into a robe with a man in it. At first it was like peering

121

through the bottom of a beer bottle, but as the sphere dissolved, the distortions unravelled and the scene became real; no, not real, but super-real, modelled in deep, rich colours with a patina like that produced by many layers of varnish matured over hundreds of years. We were gazing at the old master himself. He wasn't anything like as old as the picture in the brochure, though, not even forty, I'd say. The end of his beard was tucked into his mouth, and he was sucking it as he drew a scalpel across a rat's throat.

A boy near me retched, and the man looked up, clearly angry at being disturbed. My mammy may be Irish (that's why I've got an Irish name), but Da's Italian, and I can tell you that what Leonardo said was not fit for children's ears. We weren't in Disneyland, that's for sure. The smell, for one thing. There was a chamber pot under the table, and a bucket with contents that squirmed – lizards, leeches and suchlike, as far as I could make out. Through the chiaroscuro, a streak of chrome-yellow sunshine encircled a dead raven; the bird was pinned to a drawing board, its wings fanned out on either side of the hanging head in grim echo of a crucifixion. I could see some kids wished they hadn't come.

But not me. As a queue of autograph hunters formed, I pushed my way through to the front.

'Can I go first and translate?' I asked Mr O'Connor. 'I do know some Italian.'

'All right, Mick,' he said grudgingly, 'but remember, Signor Vinci is a genius. A little respect, if you please.'

It's true, I've no use for respect; I think I'm as good as anyone, except, perhaps, Kevin. I walked down the steps and onto the stage. The stinking heat enveloped me, as thick as honey.

Leonardo leaned one elbow on the table, cheek resting on the palm of his right hand, while he signed with the other. He yawned.

'Could you put "To Tracy, wishing you all the very best", please? It's for my friend.' I translated this for Maureen, and for Craig I translated 'What GCSEs do you need to be an artist, and what's the salary?'

I was surprised to learn your man's paid by Celebrity Tours.

''Twas not bad at first,' he told me, 'a handful of scholars researching their theses. Collecting my laundry lists, *per esempio*. But *mamma mia*, now there may be a hundred *turisti* at one time!'

Kevin handed over his sketchbook for signing. It was the one with the storyboard for 'A Comprehensive Massacre' which we'd been working on, and included the skinning of the headmaster. Leonardo flicked through the pages, then he turned them slowly, studying each drawing. He looked up at Kevin, and the boredom had left his eyes.

'*Bellissimo!*' he cried. '*Eccellente!* But how may statues move?'

We explained, as far as we were able, about latex, animation and electronically controlled, computer-programmed creatures. At this, the queue, which had shortened when the buffet opened, vanished altogether. Even Mr O'Connor had gone for a cup of tea.

Leonardo leaned across the table confidentially. 'To amaze my visitors,' he whispered, 'I once did take a lizard and cover its body with scales filled with quicksilver, then attached wings and little horns, to make a dragon. And I have, with much difficulties, made creatures from wax and entrails that I could inflate and release, and they would fly.'

'Flying's really difficult,' I said, and showed him my vampire janitor in the drawings for the disembowelling scene. His hands twisted together.

'*Un segreto!*' he said, getting up. He put a finger to his lips. Then he lifted the hem of his robe and made his way through the debris to a brocade curtain.

'This chamber is for the robing of my models,' he said, and drew us inside. It was a thicket of velvet gowns. We pushed through them, and came to a large carved chest. A chicken dozed there, head under wing, and Leonardo poked at it with a paintbrush. As the hen tumbled in a pock-pocking whirr of feathers, he lifted the lid of the chest.

Inside was a tray of tools, which Leonardo lifted and placed on the floor. 'Have you tried – ' Kev was saying, when we saw the container below. This one was partitioned. There were about ten lead-lined sections, and each section held its own display; there were hands or ears, eyeballs, noses arranged by size. There were lungs and livers, trembling like raspberry jelly, beside the hearts and brain. There was a box of toes, and one of fingers.

'The nethermost tray bears ice,' Leonardo explained. 'Mine own contrivance for the preserving of parts.' He removed two more layers, adding, 'And here I keep the whole, whereof the parts are taken.'

Two, no, three bodies, at least, lay piled one on another, and four or five more were stacked side by side. I tried to look away, but it was as if my vision had zoomed into close-up, focusing against my will on those faces, enlarging them to such huge proportions that they were a landscape in which I was trapped; I observed the way the parched yellow uplands of their features descended to verdant green in the ravines and hollows; the way the rictus of death had dragged lips in ridges around the boulders of their teeth, and eyes had sunk to become dark, unreflecting pools.

Leonardo took my hand. 'The only path to the understanding of nature is dissection. All else is childish scribble.'

'Surely you aren't allowed to keep dead bodies at home?' I exclaimed thickly, looking away. I wished I'd taken travel pills.

'That is so. I risk all in the pursuit of truth.'

Kevin gripped the edge of the chest. 'Can I stay? Will you teach me?'

'You would be apprenticed?' Leonardo asked him.

'Yes.'

'To clean the studio and empty slops, and all manner of foul work?'

'Yes!'

'But *il turista* will not return without you.'

Kevin chewed his thumbnail, then said, 'Mick, do you remember Manfred and Dieter?'

'Manfred with the long overcoat,' I said, pulling myself together. 'You mean the student-exchange scheme – What are you doing?'

He seemed to be undressing.

'You'll have to help me, Mick.' He leaned into the chest and grasped a corpse by the elbow.

'Ah, no. Not an exchange!' Gingerly, I touched the other arm. It wasn't that bad, really, smooth and cool like marble. 'You're crazy,' I said in disgust.

'Quickly. We've no time!'

I slipped my fingers underneath, and we began to lift. The legs unfolded and concertinaed over the edge of the chest. Then we sat the body down, wedged between the feet of an easel. Kevin pushed the arms into his shirtsleeves and then into his Kilkenny Comprehensive blazer. When he'd buttoned the shirt he looped his tie round the neck and tightened it. The head jerked forwards over his shoulder, and its solitary eye met mine with a vague, mild expression. Unreproachful. It didn't even blink as a fly slid round its glossy curve.

'This is a terrible idea,' I said, watching Kevin put on jerkin and hose. 'What about your family?'

'I've got eight brothers and sisters. It would be a blessed relief for them to get shot of one of us. And this is the opportunity of a lifetime, I can't let it go.'

'What about me, then? Jaysis, ye're quite happy to swan off and never see me again, and our film not made, and all our plans flown out of the window!'

'Calm down, Mick. Let's be realistic. You know we'll never actually ever get to make a film – I'll end up in the factory making light bulbs, you'll be selling ice cream with your da. But this is serious stuff, this is the genuine McCoy. Don't wimp out now. Stay with me. That is, if you'll take us both, sir.'

Leonardo handed me a smock. 'Make haste, before the fools return.'

I never could stand up to Kevin. Besides, what would I do without him? Reluctantly I changed my clothes and helped him drag two dissection

126

specimens over to the front row. We lifted them into a pair of seats, leaning against each other. What with the dim light and the peaked caps you couldn't tell they'd been dead for months – nor that they hadn't enough organs between the pair of them to make one decent human being.

Behind the curtain, we listened as the tourists went back to their places. Leonardo strode across the stage to wish them farewell. He bowed, and the trippers (apart from two) waved back. The timeship shuddered, melting away into the future.

We walked out into the studio and looked about us. There were wooden panels and canvases propped against a wall, tables with pots of primrose, carmine and cobalt blue. In the corner, a lutenist played a tune which mingled with the street cries drifting through the window. The air hummed with the smell of turpentine, roast pig, chamber pot and rotting flesh. It was a heady mixture.

But I'd not had a chance to think the whole thing through properly. I suppose I'd hoped we could stay a week or two, then Kevin might be persuaded to go home with me on another flight. The problem is, there hasn't been another flight since ours, which was over a year ago. They must have thought the corpses were us and, in consequence, banned time travel as being too dangerous.

Never mind. Despite everything, it's turned out to be the year of my life. I wouldn't want to go back now. At first I loathed it – I'm the sort of person who hates holidays, for a start, and the food and sanitation appalled me. I missed my parents, and blamed Kevin for everything. Jealousy was a factor, I must admit. I couldn't, for instance, master fresco painting the way Kevin had. The plaster kept slipping off, and once, when we had a commission in a monastery, I prepared the wrong wall so that the mural ended up with a door in the middle. But Kevin could do no wrong. *Il padrone* would ruffle his hair or pinch his cheeks – 'you paint like an angel, little Kevin' – and let him paint backgrounds, while I was still grave-robbing.

Then the day came when we constructed the wings. They measured three *braccia* across and were made from goat gut stretched over willow boughs. Kevin had worked out a way of making the joints move, using goose bones.

'Can I try them, master?' I begged. 'After all, it was me who stole the goat. And the goose.'

'Some must serve humbly,' Leonardo admonished, 'while others soar to glory.'

So I got up early the next morning to pack bread and wine in a pouch, and bind the wings into a bundle. I gave Kevin and the master their breakfast, and we set off to Mount Ciceri. It was still dark as we left Florence and made our way through the misty olive groves. Eventually we broke through the cloud cover into fresh blue air.

We climbed, the dry turf crumbling from the rock the higher we got. At noon we sat and ate our food. Then Kevin stood up and stretched out his arms. We dropped the harness over his head and fastened the straps; I checked them, wrist to shoulder.

He raised his arms, swishing the wings, beating them powerfully, carving figures of eight through the air. The willow twigs crackled as the joints flexed. Kevin turned to face the sun. His red hair foamed about his face, the freckles shone bright as gold dust; and as the wings leaped in gothic curves

he did, at last, look like an angel. He smiled at us and began to run. We saw him at the skyline, then he was gone. We crawled on our bellies and peered into the dizzying void, but he was nowhere to be seen. Hundreds of metres below, clouds turned.

'He has flown to heaven,' Leonardo sadly said. And so we went home.

I miss Kevin. Still, it's good to be out of his shadow. I'm learning more every day – perspective, anatomy, glazes, silverpoint – and though I'll never be as good as Kevin, I reckon if I keep at it, one day I'll rival the old feller. He says to me, ruffling my hair, 'Michael, you paint like an angel'; then he pinches my cheeks – 'my little Michael of the angels.'

And you must admit, as a name for a great artist, Michelangelo Buonarroti sounds a sight better than Kevinangelo Murphy.

THE FINAL WORD

I suppose he got away with it because he made the others laugh. 'Where's Snow White and the other six?' he'd ask, or 'Who sawed your legs off?' Not that such remarks are funny anyway, especially when repeated twenty times a day. The silly thing is, Max was even shorter than me. He'd got a very tall hairdo like a bog brush, and a weird way of walking on his toes which made him temporarily taller. For me, small's no problem. Max was my problem.

On the day it happened, he'd been sniggering with the boys at the back of the class. I wasn't paying any attention till he said loudly, 'I'm sure I saw a mouse. Eeny-weeny squeaky thing. Let's exterminate it.' Something slithered across the floor and flipped off my rucksack; there was a flash, an ear-numbing crack, and I lurched backwards, hitting my head on the desk behind as my chair fell. Sitting up, I heard the inane electronic chant of Max's key ring, squawking like a ventriloquist's dummy, 'You're an bleephole, bleep you, bleeping jerk.' Except it didn't say 'bleep'.

'Are you OK?' Livvy picked up my chair and

yelled at Max, 'You're the jerk. Don't you know any better than to throw fireworks? You could have blinded Sara!'

'Bleep you,' said the key ring. Max always plays it when he thinks he's pulled a good one; it's an extension of his psyche, that little black box, it's his familiar. I said nothing. I've learned better.

We walked over to lunch planning Livvy's Guy Fawkes party, and I'd almost forgotten Max till I saw him in the queue. Livvy nudged me and pointed at the talking key ring. It was dangling from his rear pocket. I glanced up and down the line – none of the boys was there, so I tapped the shoulder of the kid in front of me and nodded towards Max. The message passed along the line, and we craned our necks to watch the girl behind him carefully, oh so gently, extract the keys. It was like a scene from *Oliver!* (Though in our lunch hall no starving child, having once tasted the food, would ever cry, 'Please, sir, can I have some more?') Hand to hand, the keys travelled back to me.

Max turned – there was a wave of anguished mirth – looked puzzled and felt his pockets. I was gazing innocently at the floor, so I didn't see who it was that got thumped.

After school I rushed home and started getting the guy ready for the party; that was my contribution, as I didn't have any money for fireworks. Mum and Dad were still at work, so I was able to get some good stuff. There was a dressing gown of Dad's. He doesn't wear hats, but I found the one with poppies on it which Mum wears to weddings – it looked hilarious combined with a rubber Freddy mask. Then I stuffed a tracksuit and squashed it into the old baby buggy. I was just fixing the gloves when the bell rang.

'Come and see this, Livvy,' I said, as I opened the door. 'The funniest guy you ever – '

It was Max.

'You've got 'em, haven't you?' he snarled. 'My keys. My special novelty key ring.'

I tried to shut the door, but he was leaning against it. His tadpole eyes were an inch below mine, and my nostrils filled with the sickly perfume of hair gel.

'Push off,' I said. 'I don't know what you're talking about.'

'Don't even think of messin' me about, I know you've got 'em. It's a cold night. I can't get in my house. Just give 'em.'

My feet were sliding as the door scraped inwards. Abruptly I let go, and scrambled for the stairs. I heard Max fall into the hall as I fled upwards, two stairs at a time, dragging myself by the banisters. Looking back, I glimpsed the sawn-off haircut clambering over the buggy at the foot of the stairs. I swung into the bathroom and closed the door, softly sliding the bolt across. There was a rushing pad of feet on staircarpet, a squeak of hand on banister. The footfall advanced, retreated, as Max prowled through the bedrooms. I heard the click of wardrobe doors. I should have given the keys back straight away, I thought. It seemed possible that my instinct to run had been ill-judged.

I took the keys from my pocket and examined the black oblong on the chain. There was a square button in the centre, with a copperplate inscription: 'The Final Word'. Irresistibly, my finger was drawn to it. Instantly, piercingly, a high-pitched

American accent snapped, 'Scumbag!' The footsteps outside the door paused; an outline fogged the frosted door panels.

The handle rattled, and I shrank back into the corner between the basin and the bath. There was a thud as he kicked the door; a screw dropped from the bolt. Another thud, a massive one, as his whole body hit the door. The bolt held, but a panel shattered. Max's arm thrust through the bright star of broken glass, groping with clumsy, blind touch for the bolt. His thumb pushed it back, smearing red across the white paintwork. The door juddered open.

'All right,' I said, holding out the keys. 'If you can't take a joke . . .'

'A joke, eh?' he said, pocketing them. 'You think I like a lot of silly little girls tittering at me in the lunch hall?'

He took a handful of hair and jerked my head back. It was a surprise to me that you can feel terrified and angry at the same time. I kicked out and he let go. I ran out on the landing, but he caught up with me at the top of the stairs. Putting one arm round the newel post, with my free hand I gave him an almighty shove.

He teetered for a moment, then plunged, hands outstretched, down the stairs. At first he somersaulted, that foul mouth a recurring hole in the white face, the hands ratatatting against the banister struts before his body bounced against the wall, slithered the last few steps and struck the hall floor. That smack of cheek on tile had the sharp finality of a slap across the face, but I hugged the post and waited. I've seen enough of those films where you think the psycho's dead, then he jumps

134

up again.

But Max didn't jump up. He didn't move at all. I sat on the top step listening to the silent house, the distant battle cries of rockets. The kitchen door curved open a crack, and our cat slunk through. Head down, she approached Max. Circling, crouching, she sniffed curiously, then began to lick the blood from around his mouth. She was purring.

'Stop that,' I shouted. 'Get off.' I pulled myself together and ran down the stairs to shove her through the door, then turned to study Max. He was very pale. Very still.

What do they do with child murderers? Not hanging any more, I don't think. Possibly not even prison. Perhaps we're just sent away for ever to some sort of centre for juvenile offenders. It was difficult to think straight with panic roaring in my ears.

If I could only shift Max out of the house, everything would be all right. Off the premises, out of the area, out, out . . . But how to do it unseen? And how would I carry him? How could I even get him past the pushchair which was blocking the hall?

I started to giggle hysterically. Then my mind cleared. The most important thing was to cover Max's face, so I pulled the Freddy mask down over it. Actually, I've never seen anything quite as masklike as Max's own face, but the eyes, as in a good portrait, seemed to follow me about the room.

I forced his arms through the dressing-gown sleeves and hauled him into the buggy. Not easy, this, as it kept rolling away. When his feet were on the footstrap, his knees folded up as high as his chin. I let the chin balance on the knees while I wrapped my scarf round the neck and tied it to the handles.

136

The head was at least upright now, if a little wobbly. I put the hat on top. It was when I was pulling on the gloves that the bell rang again.

I squealed. This was the exact point where the bell had rung when I was making the first guy. I kept very still, and waited for whoever it was to go away.

'Hurry up, Sara!' came Livvy's voice. 'We know you're there. We heard you.'

Slowly I opened the door. Half the second form were standing outside.

'I don't think I can come,' I said. 'I've got a bit of a headache. Maybe later.'

'That's a shame. It'll be fun. We're going down the mall to raise money for more fireworks.'

'Oh, cool. Well, 'bye then.' I started to close the door.

'Hang about.' Livvy pushed her way in. 'We need the guy, don't we.' She took a step back to admire it. 'Wow! What a scream! It's so grotesque, you know who it reminds me of? Max. We'll call it Max.'

She took the handles and steered it through the door. The kids outside whooped when they saw him.

'Look,' I said desperately. 'He's not quite finished. Why don't I bring him in half an hour?'

'Nonsense! He's totally brilliant already.' She wheeled him away down the path. There was nothing I could do but run after her.

'Actually, I'm feeling much better,' I said, and reached across to take the handles. 'He's my guy,' I said. 'I'll push him.'

'He may not be a movie star,' Livvy sang as we walked along the road, 'but when it comes to being

137

happy – we are,' and the others joined in, 'There's not a man alive can take me away from my guy.' They seemed to think this was funny; they were clearly in a party mood. Myself, I felt like Macbeth at the feast.

Probably you've never done anything really bad; if not, then you cannot imagine the sick horror of it, the remorse, the wishing you could rewind time; knowing that if the tiniest of your actions in the last six hours had been the slightest bit different, then this one vast blot on your life would never have happened.

We threaded through the car park to the mall. The Christmas decorations were up already, with a frieze of reindeer over the entrance. I bumped Max up the steps, and the poppies on his hat danced, their petals reflecting the fairy lights. As the automatic doors slid back, I was thinking, it was self-defence; what else could I have done? A little voice in my head answered, 'You didn't have to kill him. And it must be your fault, or you wouldn't feel so bad.'

Livvy whispered, 'Watch it – there's a policeman by the fountain.'

'Oh, God,' I moaned. 'You know. How did you find out?'

'Because I can see him. What's with you tonight, Sara? He won't throw us out if we do our scrounging round the corner.'

I always feel guilty when I see a policeman. This time I stared ahead and pushed the buggy briskly past him. The little voice in my head was nagging, 'And besides, innocent people don't try to dispose of the corpse.' Max rocked with the increased speed, and one leg slipped off the footrest, the foot dragging beneath the buggy. I stooped and lifted it back into position.

'That's a mighty fine guy you've got there!' called the policeman. 'Best I've seen all night. I hope you know the bylaws, though. No begging in a public place.'

'Yes, sir,' I said hoarsely. He walked towards us, his boots rapping on the marble. We stood back as he bent down and peered at Max.

'It's very realistic. You got a kid in there?' He prodded the body, and one arm flopped over the side of the buggy.

'Perhaps not.' He laughed. The arm was certainly bent at a very peculiar angle. I tucked it back and marched on.

'You look terrible,' said Livvy, catching up. 'Do you want to go home?'

'Don't worry about me,' I said and stationed the buggy outside Tulley's, putting the brake on. 'Penny for the guy,' I called out.

For some reason, German tourists are the most generous. The English tend to say 'No, thank you', as if you're selling something, or 'Of course. If it was a good cause – but I bet you lot aren't even going to spend it on fireworks.' So I was surprised how well we did. Perhaps there was something in my face. 'Poor little thing!' one woman muttered, as she gave us five pounds. I was miles away, remembering previous Guy Fawkeses, Halloweens, Christmases; I'd been a child, then.

We'd made about twenty pounds when we spotted the policeman coming down the escalator, so Livvy bought some fireworks, and we left.

'Look,' I said. 'I've been thinking. This is my mum's wedding hat. I'll be in such deep shit if anything happens to it. Same with the dressing gown. So I'll just drop the guy off at our garage. I mean, we've got some excellent fireworks.'

'Sara, you cannot have a bonfire without a guy, and Max is the best ever. Blame me, say I nicked them. Anyway, I can't believe anyone would be seen dead in a hat like that!'

Livvy's reckless, she doesn't care about consequences. It's me who's the quiet, considerate one, who never does anything wrong. The unassertive one. So, as usual, I gave in.

'About time!' her mum greeted us, through a mouthful of nails. She was standing on a beer crate, pinning Catherine wheels to a tree. Everything managed to look normal, while in fact being an uncontrollable nightmare. There would be no waking up; I had to see it through.

'Sausages?' someone cried. The garden was spot-lighted by moving torches. Behind the house, a fiery geometry of spirals and arcs chalked the black sky. I bit into a hot dog and felt the skin burst between my teeth, filling my mouth with flesh. I saw them lift Max from the pushchair and place him on top of the bonfire. His head lolled on his chest, tipped sideways. Livvy's dad lit a taper and bent to the crumples of newspaper between the planks. Fire crept through the crevices, tangled upwards in silky ropes and bound the hulk in light. I wiped the sting of mustard from my lips.

The guy flopped high on the wood stack. His dressing-gown cord trailed the boards, and where it dangled into the flame, I watched the tassel light, watched the fire, red and sparking, crawl along its fuse. I did not like to look at his face. Shadows on the mask squirmed in and out of the wrinkles, prancing up from the sharp nose. Further down, flames from an old rabbit hutch sucked at his feet. Then the dressing gown caught, and there was a cheer from the crowd. I shuddered, but didn't look away. He blazed like the sun. The bonfire timbers creaked and shifted, and a spray of sparks splashed out. The guy's left arm slid across his chest. Then the other arm twitched. It rose feebly, and sank. Then it lifted again, fingers splayed, and clutched at the mask.

Someone screamed. The glove convulsed, now, fingers fluttering, tugging at the rubber. Guests ran at the fire, but the guy was too high, too engulfed in flame.

'Get the hosepipe,' Livvy's dad shouted.

A shriek came, as if in reply, a thin, high thread of a screech from somewhere deep inside the fire, clacking out a string of repeated phrases like some chant or prayer. Then, as the fire gnawed harder, a waft of melting plastic reached us, and the words distorted as they rose in pitch – 'Jerk . . . jerking ass . . . flup . . . fing . . . hole' – and faded away.

 he pilgrim journeyed
for many a year over
desert and mountain...

ntil he came to the monastery where the master was putting the finishing touches to his life's work. The pilgrim knocked loudly...

And went in.